D0873893

THE TRUSTING
AND THE MAIMED

THE TRUSTING
AND THE MAIMED

AND OTHER IRISH STORIES BY

JAMES PLUNKETT

WOOD ENGRAVINGS BY JOHN DE POL

THE DEVIN-ADAIR COMPANY
NEW YORK / 1955

PRINTED IN THE UNITED STATES OF AMERICA

CANADIAN AGENTS: THOMAS NELSON & SONS, TORONTO

Library of Congress Catalog Card No. 55-7741

CONTENTS

THE TRUSTING
AND THE MAIMED

THE TRUSTING
AND THE MAIMED

A T ABOUT eleven o'clock the pigeon came slowly and uncertainly from the west, leaving behind it the rim of
encircling mountains. Its wings beat heavily. It flew low. Some
miles to the east the sandy surface of a road broke the monot-
ony of the moors. The pigeon hovered. There was no movement
anywhere; no small whitewashed houses with windows to flash
as they returned the sun; no men bending their backs in labour
over the harvest, no loaded carts swaying and trundling behind sweating horses. All that lay behind. Eastwards, where
the pavements began, were the serried hall doors, the spires
and factory chimneys, the smoke and hustle which was home.
The pigeon desired the city, not this wilderness; these
worked-out turf cuttings with water too black to reflect the
sun, this marshy ground too poor to bear anything but heather
and reeds and an odd cluster of purple frocans. The pigeon
distrusted the moor, the absence of life, the silence. But its
wounded leg throbbed more painfully, its wings beat with de-
creasing strength. When suspicion and fear could no longer
sustain it, it dropped quietly to earth and began to push a pas-
sageway into the tangled heather. Under the thick growth was

9

the darkness of a smaller and more tangible world. It was companionless without the exuded warmth of other pigeons but it was bounded like the pigeon hutch at home. It gave an illusion of safety. The pigeon rested, waiting for its strength to return, every instinct yearning and quivering for the city.

From the top windows of the Georgian house the mountains which encircled the moor were clearly visible, but Florrie, busy sweeping the top landing, hardly noticed them. She had other things on her mind. Sweat had left a thin ring of dirt around the nape of her neck and made dark smears down her plump young arms. The deliberate banging of her sweeping brush against the bedroom door had failed to bring any response. The failure irritated her. She leaned across the banisters. Warm, unpleasant odours from the kitchen rose unremarked about her flushed face. It was the boarding house odour she had grown up with. Behind her, in the sunlight shafting from the window, dust swam wildly.

"Ma," she yelled.

"What is it?"

"Mr. Casey isn't stirring, Ma."

"Then for the love of God go and rouse him," her mother screamed back. "Tell him it's eleven o'clock. He'll be sacked out of his office."

Florrie bundled her hair under her kerchief and retied it before selecting the key for the door. She was used to them all—the junior clerks from insurance offices, the lonely, elderly men with no known occupation, the university students who had lived in bed-sitting rooms in her mother's house for as long as she could remember. Without embarrassment she pushed the door open. The bed which had not been slept in stopped her short in the doorway like an affront; the fact that after all the banging and the brushing there was nobody there over-awed her. A set of underwear and a soiled shirt, bundled roughly for Monday's laundry, lay in the corner. She looked enquiringly from the picture of St. Rita, patroness of hopeless cases, to a glossy photograph of a pin-up girl in a swim suit and then to a family group of Casey in a sailor's suit, sitting on a table which stood between his mother and father. On the dressing table, between a crushed tie and a sticky bottle of hairdressing, lay an envelope. Florrie picked it up, detected the faint odour of perfume, and sat down on the bed to read. Some time later, when her sweeping brush slid sideways and fell, she paid no attention.

Dear Joe,

After I got home last night I just couldn't sleep the words we had and no sign yet although it's nearly eight weeks now. Ma asked me where I was I suppose my face looked a fright was I crying a lot. You upset me talking about those people you want me to see on Monday. Joe please understand I just can't do it. It was bad enough taking those pills but what you suggest now is something so terrible it's against everything against the law and against the church. If you loved me there is a way out even now but you don't. I realise that and that makes it even more awful. I'm in this trouble because I loved you I suppose I was a fool in the first place. But I won't see those men although I think now mother is beginning to suspect something or will soon. I will get this to you by hand or somehow and please Joe see me tomorrow so that we can talk

In haste,

Rita.

Florrie rose quietly and went out once more to the landing. In the shifting sunlight dust no longer swam.

"Ma."

"What is it now?"

"Come up, Ma. Mr. Casey's not here."

"Not there."

"No, Ma. I think . . . I think he's done a bunk."

Florrie anticipated with accuracy the sudden flurry of ascending feet.

By the hour of eleven the office of Pigott & Turrow had settled down to the dusty routine of the day. It was a small office at the top of the building and from its windows also the mountains were visible. Across a jumble of roofs and chimney pots their tranquil shapes rose blue and clearcut in the autumn sunshine. The small office was quiet. Rita Kilshaw bit her lip over the letter she was attempting to type and made more mistakes than usual. After each sentence she breathed "Dear God, don't let it happen, please don't let it happen," because she hoped if she said that often enough it really wouldn't happen. She had cried so much these past few weeks that by now the relief of easy tears was no longer left to her. But the small pale hands which seemed always to be smudged with carbon seldom stopped fidgeting. She had developed the habit of drawing the corner of her lip between her teeth and looking up miserably under arched eyebrows at images which passed from time to time before her mind. She looked around sometimes at the grey head of Miss Bates as it bent over the work of the day, or said, "Yes, Mr. Turrow," in a gulping voice when the large bulk of her boss materialised beside her. There were moments of terror when she believed they knew all about it, that their voices were engaging her in conversation only that their eyes might search the lines of her body the more diligently. In the middle of her third attempt at the letter before her she stopped and opened the petty cash box. She said, trying to pitch her voice casually: "We've run rather short of stamps, Miss Bates. Do you think I should slip out for some?" Miss Bates, a little surprised, raised her head and stared at a straight, uncommunicative back.

"Can't you get them as usual on your way to lunch?"

"I suppose so."

Miss Bates, catching the note of defeat in her voice, asked with customary kindness.

"Did you want to go out for something else?"

"I've such a splitting headache," the girl lied, "I thought some fresh air might clear it."

Miss Bates, ironically misconstruing the headache, said pleasantly: "Get the stamps by all means and call at the chemist on your way."

The girl took off her overall and went down a flight to wash. Through the open window of the toilet, which looked out over a flat zinc roof at the weathered brick of walls and chimney stacks, pleasant autumn odours of the city stole in, a breeze astringent with the smell of the sea and the smoke of burning leaves in public parks. The girl examined her face in the mirror for reassurance that it was hers, that it betrayed nothing more than tiredness, bit her lip and arched her eyebrows and asked herself if she was going mad. She would have liked to have gone mad, to have escaped into sickness and fever. But the thoughts tapped out rationally and logically, as clear-cut as the zinc roof and the chimney pots, miserably sane. She took up her handbag, went through the hall which always smelled coldly of garbage, and found herself in the street.

"For you," Higgins said, pitching the instrument neatly into the tray in front of Ellis. Ellis, startled by the bump, looked up irritably from his work.

"Who is it?"

"Some bird," Higgins conveyed.

"What bird?" Ellis insisted putting his hand over the receiver. "Why the hell don't you get a name?"

"Some mutual bird," Higgins explained. "She asked for Casey—then for you."

Ellis, glancing down the office before answering, guessed the caller before he heard the voice. No views of distant mountains troubled the air-conditioned comfort of the Municipal Insurance Office, no windows allowed the sunlight to challenge the discretion of its artificial lighting. Telephones, when they rang, did so with regulated emphasis. Ellis addressed himself reluctantly to the instrument in his hand.

"Oh Rita, hello. Yes, this is Bob Ellis. No—not so far. I don't know. He didn't send in any word either. No, it's not like him. Did you try his digs? Yes, call me back and let me know. Good luck."

Ellis cut off, considered thoughtfully, and requested another number. During the second conversation he frowned and looked around two or three times at the vacant chair. He left down the receiver again and sauntered down the office, sedulously avoiding the eye of Mr. Pringle, the Chief Clerk. Pringle, Ellis knew, was deeply wounded by Casey's non-appearance. It was unbusinesslike, it was not worthy of the high tradition of the Accident Department. But Ellis, lacking an explanation, lifted the hinged leaf of the counter and tried to convey by the expression on his face that the business of the Municipal was absorbing his whole attention. He made his way past the serried desks with their serried batons of fluorescent lighting and found Connolly leaning against a filing cabinet in the Whole Life Department.

"I want to talk to you," he said.

Connolly, gravely regarding a sheet of figures which he held in his hand, asked: "Have you something good for the Curragh?"

"Not bloody horses," Ellis answered, "something serious."

"Horses are serious," Connolly said. "I dropped a tenner at Leopardstown on Saturday on a flaming certainty Higgins gave me. Every penny I could borrow."

Ellis, ignoring him for a moment, measured interrogatively the space which separated them from the nearest clerk, and dropped his voice.

"Your man Casey hasn't turned in this morning. I 'phoned his digs a while ago but the skivvy only knows his bed hasn't been slept in."

"What do you suspect?"

"I'm uneasy. The two of us have an appointment for tonight with the crowd I was telling you about."

"The crowd who were to do the what-you-may-call-it?"

"Exactly."

"And the woman—is she willing to chance it?"

"I don't know. Casey was to put it to her on Saturday and let me know to-day. He can't expect me to meet them on my own. It's dangerous. I don't mind being a friend, but I'm not going to be made a scapegoat. I'm wondering should I chance asking the woman about it myself."

When Connolly continued to regard him silently he added: "It's a bit embarrassing."

"Take my tip," Connolly said at last, "steer clear of it."

"But what about the woman. She's just been 'phoning me?"

"Is the poor bitch terrified?"

"Naturally," Ellis said. But the contempt in the question angered him. He liked the girl.

"Let her go to hell," Connolly said. "What do you want to get mixed up in it for? It's highly dangerous. And it's immoral. It's bloody immoral. You know what'll happen if you're caught."

"I know. But I'm sorry for the woman. She's a nice girl."

"That's Casey's affair."

"I wish to God he was here." Ellis said miserably. "It's a bit thick leaving me to carry the baby."

Connolly looked at him with disapproval. "An unfortunate expression," he said finally.

Later in the morning Pringle spoke to him.

"Mr. Casey has not reported for duty. Do you know anything about him?"

"No, Mr. Pringle," Ellis said. "I expect he's ill."

Pringle looked at the clock on the far wall.

"Extraordinary," he said.

The expression, Ellis gathered, was intended to convey that no word to that effect had been received although it was now fifteen minutes past twelve.

"Perhaps he could get nobody to bring a report in," Ellis offered lamely. "He may be seriously ill."

"I should hope so," Pringle said, "it seems the only charitable explanation."

The interview was cut short through Higgins' intervention.

"A telephone call for Mr. Ellis," he said apologetically to Pringle. When they got out of earshot Ellis said: "Who is it?"

"The same bird," Higgins said. "You know you ought to do your courting in your own time."

With sudden venom Ellis said.

"It's Casey's bloody bird."

"That only makes it worse, doesn't it?" Higgins answered, smiling.

II

After the fluorescent lighting Ellis found the October sunlight strong and irritating. He fretted at the delay when he was held up at traffic crossings and wondered why he had been such a fool as to ask her to lunch in the first place. But when he joined her in Stapley's he knew the answer. Rita Kilshaw was a nice girl. She was petite and dark with a childlike air which moved him tenderly. He had met her first at a hop in the tennis club but Casey had won the day. Casey was more enterprising and besides he was two years senior. At twenty-four Ellis still felt that that counted. So he gave Casey a clear field and did the best he could with her girl friend. When the affair developed on more serious lines Rita Kilshaw became forbidden territory. Ellis was prepared to chance a lot—all the chaps in Municipal were. But where a friend had staked a claim you tried not to cut in. If he got into trouble you were expected to help him. If he wanted a loan of a dinner jacket or was stuck for a few quid, you came to his rescue. If he was in more serious trouble there was a fund of commonly available information on ways and means of putting matters right. At the worst somebody always knew somebody. Unfortunately the simple remedies had failed in the present case. Ellis, looking down at Rita Kilshaw for a moment before drawing out his chair, was bitterly sorry. It was one thing taking your fun where you could and looking for a soft thing when the mood was on you, but it was quite another when things went wrong. The girl had her family, sober, sodality-minded parents who were likely to kick up holy murder. Casey's job might be at stake, because the Board had high standards of morality. The chairman, for instance, had two sons in the Jesuits. Ellis felt the whole business was disastrous.

"Did you order?" he asked.

He was answered with a look of such detached misery that he felt suddenly chilled.

"Look," he said humbly, "I don't mean to start any silly chin-up look-on-the-bright-side business. Honest. I know how you feel."

They sat in silence. The meal was going to be a hopeless affair. He tried again.

"I know it's embarrassing," he said. "I find it embarrassing too. I mean third party and so on. I know how you feel. But we've got to talk."

Her gaze was fixed on the fork which she was jabbing lightly at the tablecloth. She said:

"He wasn't at his digs last night. They think he's gone away."

"Nonsense," Ellis said, with an attempt at conviction. "He'll turn up. I wouldn't worry about that end of it."

A waitress was hovering at his shoulder. He ordered for himself. The girl would have coffee.

"Nothing else?"

"No."

"But, Rita."

"Please . . . just coffee."

The waitress went away.

"Rita," he said, "did Joe tell you he was talking to some people?"

"He did. I told him I wouldn't see them."

"It's a chance."

"Aren't things bad enough already?"

"But this may be a way out."

"There are other ways out."

"Rita, for the love of God, don't start talking like that."

"Like what?"

"About other ways out. We've got to keep our heads." Ellis realised that once again he was involving himself. Why should he say "We?" It was Casey's jam, not his. He looked down at his plate and the food filled him with disgust. He heard the girl saying:

"I think I'm going mad."

"Rita," he said, "Casey will turn up. I'm sure of it. But in the meanwhile don't let this chance pass."

"I'm not going."

"Then what are we to do?"

She had left down the fork. Her hands were tightly clenched, her face was full of so much suffering that Ellis felt every eye in the hot, sticky restaurant must be drawn by it. He sensed a crisis approaching and felt the urgent necessity for deflecting it.

"Rita," he said, gently touching her sleeve, "please don't cry. Not here. We'll have everyone staring."

"I've no intention of crying."

He knew that was a lie. She looked like somebody who at any moment might start to scream. He sighed but said nothing. The rest of the meal passed more or less silently. He led her by crowded tables. People sweated over their food, people who came in from surrounding offices and eat always in a hurry. The clatter of knives and plates helped in its own way to set nerves on edge. It was a relief to pass out once more into sunlight, to push through lunch-hurrying crowds until they reached the river wall. She began to walk towards the dock area. They passed a public convenience and a car park packed with cars. The river wall was spattered here and there with gull droppings. Ellis, glancing at a public clock, said:

"What time have you to be back at?"

"I'm not going back."

His anxiety was now mixed with irritation. He hid it but it brought him to a standstill. She was being difficult at a time when a little mutual trust meant so much.

"You'll only make things worse, Rita."

"What do *you* care?"

She turned towards the river and looked down at the green slime which showed above the low water. A light breeze was irrelevantly stirring her hair. Ellis covered her hand gently, almost shyly, with his.

"Rita," he said, "that's not fair. After all, I don't have to get mixed up with this at all. It's dangerous for me, too. I could say it's not my business. I could walk off and say to hell with it."

"Then why don't you?"

"I don't know. I suppose because I'm a pal of Casey's. Or because I like you, Rita. Maybe I like you more than I should. I can't help that—Casey or no Casey. I asked you to lunch when I knew you were feeling pretty low."

She considered this for a moment in silence. Then without looking at him, she said: "I'm sorry. I know you don't have to do this. I'm behaving like a bitch."

"Oh, no."

"Yes, I am. It's the things that keep coming into my head. When we lived in the country we had a maid. She hid it for nine months. Then she locked the bedroom door and the baby was born. Daddy packed her off. I remember the things we said about her. About skivvies and soldiers and not being able to watch them. We thought she was dirt and what could you expect. Now I keep thinking of what she suffered in that nine months—binding herself up, not pretending when she was sick, praying that it was all a nightmare."

"Rita—If you know all that why can't you do something about it? Why won't you chance these other people?"

"No."

"I'm seeing them tonight . . ."

"No."

"Then what are you to do?"

"There are plenty of things I can do," she said, looking down at the water. He caught the look.

"Rita," he urged. Her mood distressed him.

Insulating herself in her own world once more, she said:

"You'll be late back at the office."

"And what about you?"

"I've the afternoon off. I told Miss Bates I was sick."

"Rita . . . please . . ."

"Do go."

He left her leaning against the wall. Ellis found it a little incomprehensible. If you were in trouble you had to go deeper to get out. It was undesirable, of course, but beggars couldn't be choosers. The chaps in the Municipal were often enough in trouble; over horses, over drink and not doing their work properly, and now and then, like Casey, over women. Life was a succession of small deceits and subterfuges, snatched pleasures and social inconveniences. There was only one commandment—which demanded absolute regard, the eleventh commandment— Don't be caught. The rest could be discreetly tampered with. The thought filled his mind when he arrived

back at the office and he found Casey's chair still empty. Casey
had been caught. And like the cute customer he was, Casey
had run out on them. Ellis was convinced of it.

The pigeon, having found the darkness under loose heather
reassuring, burrowed in further and was suddenly gripped
by a hand. It was Casey's hand. He made no conscious decision to grab at the pigeon; the action was automatic. But the
effort made him turn a little to one side and that hurt his injured leg. Pain twisted his face. For a moment after drawing
the pigeon towards him he was tempted to kill it, to exorcise
the pain forcibly through some act of violence. Then he
noticed that the pigeon's left leg was almost severed at the
joint. Under the raw and bloody skin a single tendon joined
it to the upper half. Its breast feathers and the leg itself were
smeared with clay and grass. The right leg, uninjured, carried
a silver ring. Casey looked down at his own broken leg and
felt his self-pity large enough to embrace the maimed pigeon
Its suffering, its fright, its heart beating with terrified warmth
and softness under his hand, took his mind for a moment away
from his own plight.

"You poor little bastard," he murmured gently. He drew the
pigeon under his jacket and with extreme caution lowered his
body again until he was stretched out on the heather, the stems
rough against the side of his face. There was grit about his lips
because he had sucked moss to ease his thirst. The sun, high
overhead, drew a warm, soft, hungry odour from the moor. A
short distance away, but too far as yet for Casey's thirst to
brace him for the almost unbearable ordeal of dragging his way
towards it, the small stream reflected the sky, a vast blueness
with one small white cloud, a slow argosy in a motionless sea.

After a night spent on the open moor, the sun had come as a

trusted friend. But its heat aggravated his thirst, its light forced him to turn his head into uncomfortable positions. Casey had not known how cold the moors could be at night, how hot in the day. The pain of his broken leg, the shock of exposure were bad enough, but the brutality of these extremes he had not reckoned on. It filled him with a new fear and called out new reserves of cunning. The other fear had been his constant companion for weeks. It followed him into the office in the morning and walked home beside him in the evening. It kept him awake in his room at night, contemplating the disastrous consequences should anything misfire in his dealing with the men Ellis knew, and the equally disastrous consequences of letting things take their course. It had become unbearable after Mass on Sunday and drove him in flight from the company of the lodgers, from the necessity of behaving as though nothing was wrong, from the misery of another depressing evening with Rita Kilshaw.

The mountains had provided some measure of peace which encouraged him to carry on across the moors. There was peace and there were no people. He had been aware, of course, that one day's respite was no solution, that the sight of the first lights stringing along the first suburban road would bring back all the suffering and indecision once more, but up to the moment when he caught his foot in the hole and pitched forward heavily he had known a calm which had not been his for weeks. It was a calm in which it had occurred to him that he might marry her after all. It would be difficult to arrange, it would be hard to find money and set up a home. But when it was all smoothed over it might work out successfully. The idea had begun to engage his serious consideration.

The pigeon stirred against his breast and he stroked it until it settled down again, accepting his friendliness now without further question, so reassured and quiet that after a while Casey forgot all about it. He closed his eyes. They would be wondering where he was, Florrie when she found his room unoccupied, Ellis when he failed to turn up at the office, Rita Kilshaw when she received no letter and no telephone call.

"Is there any change?" he had asked with growing hopelessness every day. There had been moments when he loved her wildly; when he left her home on the night of their first meeting; on the golf links when intimacy had first offered. They had spent the whole August day on the beach; swimming, throwing a beach ball from one to the other afterwards and lying lazily in the sun until the time came to make tea on the oil stoves the others had brought. Everyone shared spoons and laughed because sand had found its way into some of the sandwiches. When he wanted milk and sugar for his tea she had said, "Let me do it" in a way which gave him to understand that it was her pleasure to perform such a trivial and everyday service for him, that she was playfully attempting to transform it from ordinariness into some kind of smiling sacramental. He touched her arm as she leaned over him. It was cool and streaked intimately with fine sand. Afterwards, when the rest went on to a dance in the seaside town, they lingered behind but promised to follow.

Much later, when it was already dusk, they did so, crossing the golf links alone together. Mooncast shadows made the ground deceptive. She said to him: "Look at the moon on the sea." They stood still on the cliffs. Then without any further word they sat down. The night was soft and warm. Below them one broad path of moonlit silver cleaved the dark symmetry of the ocean. To their right, about a mile away, the curved arm of the bay winked with coloured lights, the amplifier in a fairground sent a popular tune drifting tentatively towards them over the dark interval of water. The light breeze left a salt taste which mingled with the odour of clipped grass. He kissed her. She said:

"We're going to miss the rest."

"Does it matter?"

"No."

Somewhere in the back of his head a gaily coloured beach ball was floating to and fro amid disembodied laughters, the desirable coolness of arms was streaked irresponsibly with fine white sand. All day he had been living beyond his means because it was Bank Holiday, all day acting an opulent lie. Now, becoming himself, he said with engaging modesty:

"I wish I had money."

"Haven't you?"

"A clerk in the Municipal—a clerk anywhere?"

"It's quite respectable to be a clerk."

"A salary scale starting at three quid a week and rising by annual increments over twenty-one years to a max of ten pounds. Sign the clock in at nine and sign it out at five. Three weeks' paid leave every year and a contributory pension scheme. That's being a clerk."

"Isn't there promotion?"

"Yes. If you study at night for ten years. Do your accountancy or secretarial. Go bald and lose your teeth. I want money while I'm young."

"Money is nice."

"Money is everything. Money is a yacht of your own. Money is a coloured beach ball. Money buys the sun we had to-day and the moon we have to-night. Money is short drinks in expensive hotel lounges. Money is making love to a nice girl like you."

"And to a nice boy like you."

"Rita."

She lay back in the grass and laughed. "Let's make a litany again about money," she suggested lazily.

"Rita," he repeated, and bent down to her. He took her in his arms. After a while he amended: "Money isn't everything."

"What is everything?"

Her coolness, her shapeliness, the faint fragrance of the sea clinging about her, sent the coloured ball flashing as it crossed and recrossed. She was no longer a bit of fluff or a dame or a date. He found her transformed and incredibly beautiful. "This," he had said, kissing her again. She stroked his hair. A warm voluptuous flood engulfed him.

Casey twisted without due caution and sweated again with vicious pain. "Jesus," he breathed. Pain and hunger and heat racked him with nausea. The pigeon began to flutter wildly. "Stop it," he breathed. "Give over." He had been lying still for too long in the sun. His eyes were momentarily blinded, a luminous brown blindness which terrified him. It was like trying to waken from a nightmare and not being able. He raised himself on his elbow and waited. The pigeon quietened. His eyes cleared. There was no sound but the unceasing murmur of the nearby stream. Under the arched sky with its becalmed white cloud the sun-filled moor was empty.

III

The river was now quite full. It flowed in a brown flood quietly between slime-encrusted walls and smelled of the sea. Spires and towers cluttered in smoky disorder the horizon ahead. A Franciscan church rose behind ugly railings to her right and on the opposite bank the hands of a public clock stood at five—almost tea-time. After leaving Ellis she had

walked down-river until the rattle of cranes unloading ships
warned her that the dock area was just ahead. She had turned
back and walked up-river then, pausing often to note the swirl-
ing conflict when the tide began to force its way against the
river. Gulls circled with sharp cries. Going home was out of
the question. She could not sit down at table with the family
in the drab homeliness of the kitchen to lie to them when she
was asked why she had not been home to lunch. She could not
sit listening to the radio in the front room with the holy pictures
staring at her from the walls. The water she had considered
but dismissed. There were too many people. Besides it was a
mortal sin. If she did that she would go straight to hell. She
would plunge deep down through the turmoil of river and tide
into flames and everlasting torment. So it was either home or
walk on and on or the church. While she hesitated a woman
passed her and she prayed, "Jesus, O Jesus," because the
woman was big with child. She had the habit of prayer. She
prayed the weather would be fine for the club outing and she
prayed her brother would get through his Leaving Cert, and
she prayed the pastry wouldn't burn if she made tarts on a
Sunday. She prayed to St. Anthony when she mislaid the petty
cash book in the office. He found it for her. She prayed to St.
Francis when the dog got sick and the dog got better. The
habit drove her into the church. You prayed to St. Anne for
childing mothers, but did that apply to unmarried ones? The
church was large and restfully dark, lit only by the wavering
shrine candles and the solitary lamp which burned before the
tabernacle. There was no saint now to pray to or, if there was,
she had not been informed. Having an illegitimate baby was
unthinkable. Miss Bates would tell Mr. Turrow when it all
came out and the tennis club and the social club would say
Rita Kilshaw of all people. The months would pass and she

would get bigger and bigger and they would say he thought her good enough for that but not good enough to marry. No one had told her who was the patron saint of skivvies and prostitutes. She would pray to the Sacred Heart. They got the *Messenger of the Sacred Heart* at home and it was wonderful the favours and miracles which the devotion elicited. Incurable disease disappears, job secured when all seemed hopeless, two hundred and sixty three favours notified to our office this month, father cured of excessive drinking, rent obtained and eviction notice quashed at last moment. It was all listed. She began to pray to the Sacred Heart, fervently, in short ejaculations, until the tension inside her eased and her attention began to wander. A ragged man with cord tied about his coat for a belt was doing the Stations of the Cross. A stout, heavily built friar crossed the altar, genuflected and came down the church. He had a large grey face and his pendulent rosary rattled as he walked. He carried a stole in his hand. Without ceremony he entered a confessional to her left. People moved over. She found herself rising, genuflecting and taking her place with them. She made no examination of conscience, no preliminary confessing to God, no act of contrition. She had lived with conscience and contrition for weeks. The first penitent entered. The rest moved up. Clenching her hands in the hypnotic dimness she neither prayed nor thought. She waited. Terror found an inlet, seeped through, invaded her to the fingertips. She sweated, but refrained from prayer or thought. She waited.

"I can't tell them, Father. I can't."

"What else can you do *but* tell them, my child."

"My father is a religious man. He won't have me under his roof."

"He must learn to be a more religious one and do his duty.

He must protect you and look after you in the trial ahead of you. Later on I can offer some help too."

"They'll never forgive me."

"Tell them God has forgiven you. You have made your peace. You have had absolution and you are worthy of the sacraments. If they withhold forgiveness they will render an account for it. But you must have courage, my child. You must trust in God."

"Yes, Father."

"Tell them the moment you go home. And come back to me in one week. I can help you. I can give you a note, perhaps, to the Reverend Mother of a community who do good work. They'll look after you. Now promise God, solemnly promise God in His sacrament of penance, to tell your parents!"

"I promise."

"Don't, when you feel lost and hopeless and unloved, give way to despair. The devil will tempt you often to despair and that is when you will most need God's grace and strength to help you. Remember God is your Friend. And as His priest I am here to help you too. You will come to see me again in a week?"

"I promise."

"For your penance say three *Hail Marys* and three *Glorias*. Now make a good Act of Contrition."

The penance was trivial, less than you would get for immoderate love-making or for reading an immoral book. Did it mean God took account of how she had suffered, how she would be made suffer in the months ahead? Feeling that God's compassion and His absolution flowed quietly over her through the priest, she finished her Act of Contrition and felt her lashes sticky with tears.

"Now go in peace. And pray for me."

"And . . . for me, Father?"

"God bless you, child."

The slide clicked shut. One moment a large head leaning on a huge hand, soft voice weary with the tribulation of the world. Then a blank wooden wall. Had he been there at all?

IV

Not for the first time it occurred to Casey that he might die. During the first hours of pain, during the cold of the previous night, during the unbearable heat of the early afternoon, the thought had suggested itself. He had pushed it away. It was too melodramatic, too unthinkable. He was within eight miles of the city, within eight miles of hospitals, X-ray apparatus, ambulances, of blood plasma and surgical instruments and anaesthetics. You turned on a tap and you got water, you turned a knob for music, you touched a switch for light. Eight miles was nothing; two minutes by plane, twenty slowly by car, less than an hour by bicycle. If he could walk he would be there in a little over two hours. But he could not walk because his leg was broken. It was as simple as that. He could not even reach the stream some yards away, although thirst had driven him several times to suck the moss which grew near his hand. So if nobody came this way, he would die. It seemed unlikely that anyone would, unless the weekend brought someone else hiking along the same stretch of moor. The weekend would be too late. He had no food and the nights were too damp and cold. He had seen no houses. The road was some miles ahead, but it was used by turfcutters and the turfcutting season was over. A shepherd? There had been sheep at the foot of the mountains, but not here. Casey, raised on his elbow, his arm now chilled and numbed by the damp earth, looked at his

enemy the moor, a dark and empty expanse, now silently waiting the approach of night. The lower slopes of the mountains
gleamed here and there in unaccountable light, but the sum-
mits and the sky over them were draped in rainy blackness.
A wind rippled the purple loneliness of the heather, gripped
and tossed his sleeves and the lapels of his jacket. Its coldness
attacked his courage. He looked to the west. The sun had
left an angry afterglow, a ragged sprawl of clouds and crimson
light. Looking into its glowing caverns, his heart failing, Casey
thought of God and sin and eternity. He had never outgrown
the idea that the gateways to heaven and hell were somewhere
in the sky; dreadful portals to trial and judgment which still,
as in childhood, he saw in a rent cloud or an angry sunset. He
was small and sick and maimed and mortal. The moor was
immense, the sun straddled civilizations, the sky was infinite,
like God. They were all enemies. Out of such a sunset the trumpets would blast, the Son of God in power and majesty come
signing for a Cessation. Those who went to their duties, the
daily communicants and the sodality men, the sayers of family
rosaries and the women who went to evening devotions, these
would be called in; people like Pringle and Rita Kilshaw's
father and the Chairman of the Board who had two sons in the
Jesuits. And outside would be left the dogs and the sorcerers,
the whoremongers and the fornicators. Casey knew his cate-
gory. It filled him with fear, but it moved him also with a desperate cunning. He began to weigh again the odds against
him, the possibilities of escape. He wanted desperately to escape, not so much now his pain and the indifference of the
moor, but the trumpets and the judgment, the onset of eternity
and its glowing cauldron of condemnation. God was Just, they
said, and God was Merciful. But he had always been suspicious
of the mercy end of it. He had never noticed much of it knock-

ing round, not when it came to the point. Death and eternity he would push aside and cheat. It was easy in town. If they nagged you you simply stopped thinking about them, by switching on the radio or dropping down to the social club or by figuring out a crossword. Here you did it by going over again the ways of escape. It was hard though. It was nearly impossible. He was beginning to stare at the sunset again with hopeless foreboding when the pigeon occurred to him. It was a racing pigeon—he knew that by the silver ring. It would fly for home. When you'd wings a broken leg did not matter so long as you got off the ground. Wings were a kind of double indemnity. Casey could see it got off the ground. He could throw it into the air. It was only necessary to write a note, describing where he was, stuff it into the ring, and the pigeon would deliver it. Pigeons were pretty fast.

Casey tore a page from his diary and did so. It was difficult to be anyway accurate about where he was, but what he had written would serve. He drew the pigeon from under his coat and began to insert the folded paper between the ring and the flesh. It was difficult. The ring was tight and the pigeon grew restless. He tore up what he had written and did it again, writing smaller this time so as to use less paper. It was still difficult to insert. He tried several times. When at last he got it small enough and had a quarter of its length inserted the pigeon, jerking suddenly, half freed itself, so that Casey in surprise pulled hard at the injured leg. "Wait, you bastard," he breathed. The leg tore again before he released it. His arm was almost at the end of its reach, so that the pigeon, half-thrown, rolled rather than flew into the air. It struggled, its wings flapping wildly, its leg dangling useless. But the piece of paper remained in the ring and the pigeon regained control and rose. Then, having resisted with his last effort until he saw it winging steadily towards the east, Casey fainted with the pain which his effort had cost him.

V

"Search me," Ellis said feelingly, "I've tried every pub and rendezvous in this flipping town."

"And the lassie is not keen either?" asked the big man in the bowler. He sounded gloomy and disillusioned.

"That's putting it mildly," Ellis said.

"It's clear to me," the little man with the red lump on his forehead observed, "from what this young fella has been telling us, that she's highly dangerous material anyway. And the other fella has hopped it. It's not honourable, but there it is."

"Now you have it in a nutshell," Ellis said.

The big man sighed deeply.

"Taking it by and large," he said, "I think it's healthier we called it a day."

"Me too," the little man said.

"I'm sorry," Ellis apologised.

"That's all right," the little man assured him gloomily. "You've acted honourable. It's not your fault."

"Thanks," Ellis said. "I'm glad you see it that way." They drank in silence. Then the other two left and Ellis, grateful to be alone, ordered himself a beer. From time to time Casey's cowardice made him frown and pucker his lips. He felt doubly betrayed. He had risked a lot to save him, and he had stood aside and let him have a clear field with Rita Kilshaw. But mostly he thought of Rita Kilshaw. She had not been very kind to him; she had certainly not been grateful. But he would have given her anything she asked in return for one responsive word. He hoped she would do nothing desperate. Gradually withdrawing from the smokefilled lounge he stared in alcoholic melancholy at the uncurtained window. It was dark. Blobs of rain were breaking on it into flowing rivulets. Gradually these spread until below him the lights of street standards and passing traffic began to look like melting stars.

VI

"I don't know if I can let this pass without some sort of formal report to the Board. You are extremely late. And you've broken your leg."

"I'm sorry Mr. Pringle, I was out walking when it got caught in a hole which was hidden under the bracken. I pitched forward and twisted on it. I can only assure you that it was quite unintentional."

"I must accept your word I suppose. But how did you get here?"

"At first I crawled. Then I hailed a passing pigeon, which very kindly offered me a lift. It had a leg on it and one of its rings was broken."

"I see. You know I've warned you before about coming in improperly attired. On one occasion you were wearing a pyjama jacket but you wore your tie with it in the hope it would pass as a shirt. That was outrageous."

"I believe I apologised."

"You did. And I overlooked it, which you will admit was very fair of me."

"I know, Mr. Pringle. I suppose I should go home."

"If you could even make it look a bit more tidy. The bone is sticking out through the skin. Isn't that uncomfortable?"

"It is. But when I try to put it back the pain is unbearable."

"I see."

"May I go to my desk?"

"I suppose you may. But tidy it up somehow. The Chairman of the Board may appear at any moment in great power and majesty to judge the living and the dead. We can't let him find you like this—can we? Perhaps if you happen to hear the trumpets in time you will take steps to . . . well . . . to discreetly absent yourself."

"I will, Mr. Pringle."

"In the meanwhile turn up your collar, it's beginning to rain. If you look round you will notice the rest of the staff have wisely provided themselves with heads. It keeps the rain off their umbrellas."

"But where is the roof Mr. Pringle? Has somebody taken it?"

"The roof?"

"There used to be a roof. I remember it distinctly."

"You are a little feverish, Mr. Casey."

"But there was. There ought to be a roof."

"Roof?"

"Yes, a roof. Wasn't there? Surely there was a roof?"

"No roof, Mr. Casey. Cold rain and no roof. Curl up on the floor here, I think, yes, here on the green inlaid linoleum by the thin tubular legs of this desk. Turn up your collar and curl up coldly under the cold rain. Why, Mr. Casey, you are shivering."

VII

The rain had crept in on the city just as the public lamps were being lit. It was a soft, cold curtain of rain which swung sadly over the streets and flecked noiselessly on the dark waters of the river. To Rita Kilshaw it symbolised the end of any little comfort the streets could offer. Drop by drop it adulterated and washed out forever the clinging sediment of hope. She went home. The light in the front window told her where the family had gathered. Letting herself in quietly she went straight to the kitchen. She stood for some time in the darkness, her hair wet, her bag clasped under her arm. Her thoughts were slow and confused and in the back of her head was a low incessant murmuring. She knew she had been heard. It was not possible to open the hall door and go down the narrow stairs without being heard. But though she waited tensely for some time nobody called. She repeated to herself: "He said you're to forgive me that God has already forgiven me. He said to tell you. He said God has forgiven me and that's why I'm to tell you that if God has forgiven me you are to forgive me too." But it was difficult to put it right going over it in the darkness and feeling your hair heavy and wet and your bag tight under your arm. It was difficult with the murmuring in her head incessantly dragging her from concentration. She bit her lip. She knew she looked a fright and she would shock them standing in the doorway for a while waiting for the words to come. But there was nothing else for it. As she went up the hall again the murmuring grew. She flung open the front room door. It took her some time to realise that the murmuring had not been in her head. Her father and mother and her two younger brothers and sisters were all on their knees. Her mother looked around first. They were saying the family rosary.

VIII

The pigeon met the full fury of the rain as it approached the suburbs. First the darkness had closed in and then a breeze from the right, strengthening to a wind, buffeted it. But home

was in the wind too, home and the reek of smoke, the smell of little gardens, the promise of lit windows under thousands of cosy roofs, the darkness and safety of the pigeon hutch. It struggled on. Near the end the rain almost drove it to earth again. The pigeon persisted. Darkness and rain would end with home; food and ease were within reach. It was quite dark when it reached its destination, so dark that only for the flurry of its fall and the fact that it scrambled forward noisily because of its useless leg, the boy waiting for it at the window would not have known it had arrived. He shouted to his father: "He's here. I heard him. There's something wrong." He rushed out. The pigeon, frightened by its skid, suspecting another trap, was flapping its wings blindly and fighting for balance on the muddy soil. It went round in frantic circles. When the boy caught it at last he shouted to his father: "He's hurt, Pingy is hurt."

"Bring him in," his father commanded. The boy, his hair already matted with rain, took the pigeon gently against his breast and brought it indoors. They examined the wounded leg under the kitchen light. "This is bad," the boy's father said, shaking his head, "poor old Pingy." For a while apprehension kept the boy silent. Then he asked:

"What can we do?"

"Not much," his father said. "Give him food and bind it up until the morning. Then we can do him in. Quietly.' '

"No," the boy said, "it'll mend. I won't let you."

"It's kinder that way," his father said. "He's in pain and it won't mend. It's damn nearly torn off." The boy looking at the pigeon with love, said: "Pingy."

"It won't take long," his father told him gently. "The air gun upstairs—or a twist of the neck. It'll be all over in a second. It's better than suffering."

"If I knew who done it," the boy said in sudden fury, "I'd give *them* the air gun."

He was trying not to cry. His father said nothing. He was skilfully binding the leg. Rain rattled in a tumultuous gust against the window.

"By God," the boy's father said, "that's a night and a half."

Ellis, making his way home along the wall of the river, turned up his collar and said the same thing. It startled Florrie, who was assessing for her mother the value of what was left in the tenantless room with its set of soiled underwear and its bottle of sticky hair dressing. Rain covered mountain and moor and city in an unremitting downpour. It made a torrent of the little stream, nearer which Casey now lay, his shoulders hunched, his arms across his breast, summoning his yielding and outnumbered garrison to stand desperately against this latest assault. It battered the soft earth of the garden and beat to pulp the piece of paper which the pigeon had dislodged from its ring in its first frantic efforts to find balance. It drummed loudly on the corrugated roof of the pigeon hutch. But the pigeon was undisturbed. Surrounded by familiar odours it dozed comfortably and warmly after the painful length of the day. It was fed and at ease now, and confident once more of love.

WEEP FOR OUR PRIDE

THE door of the classroom was opened by Mr. O'Rourke just as Brother Quinlan was about to open it to leave. They were both surprised and said "Good morning" to one another as they met in the doorway. Mr. O'Rourke, although he met Brother Quinlan every morning of his life, gave an expansive but oddly unreal smile and shouted his good morning with bloodcurdling cordiality. They then withdrew to the passage outside to hold a conversation.

In the interval English Poetry books were opened and the class began to repeat lines. They had been given the whole of a poem called *Lament for the Death of Eoghan Roe* to learn. It was very patriotic and dealt with the poisoning of Eoghan Roe by the accursed English, and the lines were very long, which made it difficult. The class hated the English for poisoning Eoghan Roe because the lines about it were so long. What made it worse was that it was the sort of poem Mr. O'Rourke loved. If it was *Hail to thee blythe spirit* he wouldn't be so fond of it. But he could declaim this one for them in a rich fruity, provincial baritone and would knock hell out of anybody who had not learned it.

40

Peter had not learned it. Realising how few were the minutes left to him he ran his eyes over stanza after stanza and began to murmur fragments from each in hopeless desperation. Swaine, who sat beside him, said, "Do you know this?"

"No," Peter said, "I haven't even looked at it."

"My God," Swaine breathed in horror, "You'll be mangled."

"You could give us a prompt."

"And be torn limb from limb," said Swaine with conviction; "not likely."

Peter closed his eyes. It was all his mother's fault. He had meant to come to school early to learn it but the row delayed him. It had been about his father's boots. After breakfast she had found that there were holes in both his shoes. She held them up to the light which was on because the November morning was wet and dark.

"Merciful God, child," she exclaimed, "there's not a sole in your shoes. You can't go out in those."

He was anxious to put them on and get out quickly, but everybody was in bad humour. He didn't dare to say anything. His sister was clearing part of the table and his brother Joseph, who worked, was rooting in drawers and corners and growling to everybody.

"Where the hell is the bicycle pump? You can't leave a thing out of your hand in this house."

"I can wear my sandals," Peter suggested.

"And it spilling out of the heavens—don't be daft, child." Then she said, "What am I to do at all?"

For a moment he hoped he might be kept at home. But his mother told his sister to root among the old boots in the press. Millie went out into the passage. On her way she trod on the cat, which meowed in intense agony.

"Blazes," said his sister, "that bloody cat."

She came in with an old pair of his father's boots, and he was made try them on. They were too big.

"I'm not going out in those," he said, "I couldn't walk in them."

But his mother and sister said they looked lovely. They went into unconvincing ecstasies. They looked perfect they said, each backing up the other. No one would notice.

"They look foolish," he insisted, "I won't wear them."

"You'll do what you're told," his sister said. They were all older than he and each in turn bullied him. But the idea of being made look ridiculous nerved him.

"I won't wear them," he persisted. At that moment his brother Tom came in and Millie said quickly.

"Tom, speak to Peter—he's giving cheek to mammy." Tom was very fond of animals. "I heard the cat," he began, looking threateningly at Peter who sometimes teased it. "What were you doing to it?"

"Nothing," Peter answered, "Millie walked on it." He tried to say something about the boots but the three of them told him to shut up and get to school. He could stand up to the others but he was afraid of Tom. So he had flopped along in the rain feeling miserable and hating it because people would be sure to know they were not his own boots.

The door opened and Mr. O'Rourke came in. He was a huge man in tweeds. He was a fluent speaker of Irish and wore the gold Fainne in the lapel of his jacket. Both his wrists were covered with matted black hair.

"Filidheact" he roared and drew a leather from his hip pocket.

Then he shouted "Dun do leabhar" and hit the front desk a ferocious crack with the leather. Mr. O'Rourke was an ardent Gael who gave his orders in Irish—even during English class.

Someone had passed him up a poetry book and the rest closed theirs or turned them face downwards on their desks.

Mr. O'Rourke, his eyes glaring terribly at the ceiling, from which plaster would fall in fine dust when the 3rd year students overhead tramped in or out, began to declaim:

"Did they dare, did they dare, to slay Eoghan Roe O'Neill?
Yes they slew with poison him they feared to meet with
    steel."

He clenched his powerful fists and held them up rigidly before his chest.

"May God wither up their hearts, may their blood cease
    to flow!
May they walk in living death who poisoned Eoghan
    Roe!"

Then quite suddenly, in a business-like tone, he said, "You—Daly."

"Me sir?" said Daly, playing for time.

"Yes, you fool," thundered Mr. O'Rourke. "You."

Daly rose and repeated the first four lines. When he was half-way through the second stanza Mr. O'Rourke bawled, "Clancy." Clancy rose and began to recite. They stood up and sat down as Mr. O'Rourke commanded while he paced up and down the aisles between the seats. Twice he passed close to Peter. He stood for some time by Peter's desk bawling out names. The end of his tweed jacket lay hypnotically along the edge of Peter's desk. Cummins stumbled over the fourth verse and dried up completely.

"Line," Mr. O'Rourke bawled. Cummins, calmly pale, left his desk and stepped out to the side of the class. Two more were sent out. Mr. O'Rourke walked up and down once more and stood with his back to Peter. Looking at the desk at the very back he suddenly bawled. "Farrell."

Peter's heart jerked. He rose to his feet. The back was still towards him. He looked at it, a great mountain of tweed, with a frayed collar over which the thick neck bulged in folds. He could see the antennae of hair which sprouted from Mr. O'Rourke's ears and could smell the chalk-and-ink schoolmaster's smell of him. It was a trick of Mr. O'Rourke's to stand with his back to you and then call your name. It made the shock more unnerving. Peter gulped and was silent.

"Wail . . ." prompted Mr. O'Rourke.

Peter said, "Wail. . . ."

Mr. O'Rourke paced up to the head of the class once more.

"Wail—wail him through the island," he said as he walked. Then he turned around suddenly and said, "Well, go on."

"Wail, wail him through the island," Peter said once more and stopped.

"Weep," hinted Mr. O'Rourke.

He regarded Peter closely, his eyes narrowing.

"Weep," said Peter, ransacking the darkness of his mind but finding only emptiness.

"Weep, weep, weep," Mr. O'Rourke said, his voice rising.

Peter chanced his arm. He said, "Wail wail him through the island weep, weep, weep."

Mr. O'Rourke stood up straight. His face conveyed at once shock, surprise, pain.

"Get out to the line," he roared, "you thick lazy good-for-nothing bloody imbecile. Tell him what it is, Clancy." Clancy dithered for a moment, closed his eyes and said:

"Sir—Wail, wail him through the island, weep, weep for
    our pride
Would that on the battle field our gallant chief had died."

Mr. O'Rourke nodded with dangerous benevolence. As Peter shuffled to the line the boots caught the iron upright of the desk and made a great clamour. Mr. O'Rourke gave him a cut with the leather across the behind. "Did you look at this, Farrell?" he asked.

Peter hesitated and said uncertainly, "No, sir."

"It wasn't worth your while, I suppose?"

"No sir. I hadn't time, sir."

Just then the clock struck the hour. The class rose. Mr. O'Rourke put the leather under his left armpit and crossed himself. "In ainm an atair," he began. While they recited the *Hail Mary* Peter, unable to pray, stared at the leafless rain-soaked trees in the square and the serried rows of pale, prayerful faces. They sat down.

Mr. O'Rourke turned to the class.

"Farrell hadn't time," he announced pleasantly. Then he looked thunderously again at Peter. "If it was an English penny dreadful about Public Schools or London crime you'd find time to read it quick enough, but when it's about the poor hunted martyrs and felons of your own unfortunate country by a patriot like Davis you've no time for it. You're the makings of a fine little Britisher." With genuine pathos Mr. O'Rourke then recited:

"The weapon of the Sassenach met him on his way
   And he died at Cloch Uachter upon St. Leonard's day."

"That was the dear dying in any case, but if he died for the likes of you Farrell it was the dear bitter dying, no mistake about it."

Peter said, "I meant to learn it."

"Hold out your hand. If I can't preach respect for the patriot dead into you, then honest to my stockings I'll beat respect into you. Hand."

Peter held it out. He pulled his coat sleeve down over his wrist. The leather came down six times with a resounding impact. He tried to keep his thumb out of the way because if it hit you on the thumb it stung unbearably. But after four heavy slaps the hand began to curl of its own accord, curl and cripple like a little piece of tinfoil in a fire, until the thumb lay powerless across the palm, and the pain burned in his chest and constricted every muscle. But worse than the pain was the fear that he would cry. He was turning away when Mr. O'Rourke said:

"Just a moment Farrell. I haven't finished."

Mr. O'Rourke gently took the fingers of Peter's hand, smoothing them out as he drew them once more into position. "To teach you I'll take no defiance," he said, in a friendly tone and raised the leather. Peter tried to hold his crippled hand steady.

He could not see properly going back to his desk and again the boots deceived him and he tripped and fell. As he picked himself up Mr. O'Rourke, about to help him with another, though gentler, tap of the leather, stopped and exclaimed—

"Merciful God, child, where did you pick up the boots?"

The rest looked with curiosity. Clancy, who had twice excelled himself, tittered. Mr. O'Rourke said, "And what's the funny joke, Clancy?"

"Nothing, sir."

"Soft as a woman's was your voice, O'Neill, bright was your eye," recited Mr. O'Rourke, in a voice as soft as a woman's, brightness in his eyes. "Continue, Clancy." But Clancy, the wind taken out of his sails, missed and went out to join the other three. Peter put his head on the desk, his raw hands tightly under his armpits, and nursed his wounds while the leather thudded patriotism and literature into the other, unmurmuring, four.

Swaine said nothing for a time. Now and then he glanced at Peter's face. He was staring straight at the book. His hands were tender, but the pain had ebbed away. Each still hid its rawness under a comfortably warm armpit.

"You got a heck of a hiding," Swaine whispered at last. Peter said nothing.

"Ten is too much. He's not allowed to give you ten. If he gave me ten I'd bring my father up to him."

Swaine was small, but his face was large and bony and when he took off his glasses sometimes to wipe them there was a small red weal on the bridge of his nose. Peter grunted and Swaine changed the subject.

"Tell us who owns the boots. They're not your own."

"Yes they are," Peter lied.

"Go on," Swaine said, "who owns them? Are they your brother's?"

"Shut up," Peter menaced.

"Tell us," Swaine persisted. "I won't tell a soul. Honest." He regarded Peter with sly curiosity. He whispered, "I know they're not your own, but I wouldn't tell it. We sit beside one another. We're pals. You can tell me."

"Curiosity killed the cat . . ." Peter said.

Swaine had the answer to that. With a sly grin he rejoined, "Information made him fat."

"If you must know," Peter said, growing tired, "they're my father's. And if you tell anyone I'll break you up in little pieces. You just try breathing a word."

Swaine sat back, satisfied.

Mr. O'Rourke was saying that English used treachery when

they poisoned Eoghan Roe. But what could be expected of the English except treachery?

"Hoof of the horse," he quoted, "Horn of a bull, smile of a Saxon." Three perils. Oliver Cromwell read his Bible while he quartered infants at their mother's breasts. People said let's forget all that. But we couldn't begin to forget it until we had our full freedom. Our own tongue, the sweet Gaelic *teanga,* must be restored once more as the spoken language of our race. It was the duty of all to study and work towards that end.

"And those of us who haven't time must be shown how to find the time. Isn't that a fact, Farrell?" he said. The class laughed. But the clock struck and Mr. O'Rourke put the lament regretfully aside.

"Mathematics," he announced, "Ceimseata."

He had hoped it would continue to rain during lunch time so that they could stay in the classroom. But when the automatic bell clanged loudly and Mr .O'Rourke opened the frosted window to look out, it had stopped. They trooped down the stairs. They pushed and jostled one another. Peter kept his hand for safety on the banisters. Going down the stairs made the boots seem larger. He made straight for the urinal and stayed there until the old brother whose duty it was for obscure moral reasons to patrol the place had passed through twice. The second time he said to him, "My goodness boy, go out into the fresh air with your playmates. Shoo—boy—shoo," and stared at Peter's retreating back with perplexity and suspicion.

Dillon came over as he was unwrapping his lunch and said, "Did they dare, did they dare to slay Eoghan Roe O'Neill."

"Oh, shut up," Peter said.

Dillon linked his arm and said, "You got an awful packet." Then with genuine admiration he added, "You took it super.

He aimed for your wrist, too. Not a peek. You were wizard. Cripes. When I saw him getting ready for the last four I was praying you wouldn't cry."

"I never cried yet," Peter asserted.

"I know, but he lammed his hardest. You shouldn't have said you hadn't time."

"He wouldn't make me cry," Peter said grimly, "not if he got up at 4 o'clock in the morning to try it."

O'Rourke had lammed him all right, but there was no use trying to do anything about it. If he told his father and mother they would say he richly deserved it. It was his mother should have been lammed and not he.

"You were super anyway," Dillon said warmly. They walked arm in arm. "The Irish," he added sagaciously, "are an unfortunate bloody race. The father often says so."

"Don't tell me," Peter said with feeling.

"I mean, look at us. First Cromwell knocks hell out of us for being too Irish and then Rorky slaughters us for not being Irish enough."

It was true. It was a pity they couldn't make up their minds.

Peter felt the comfort of Dillon's friendly arm. "The boots are my father's," he confided suddenly, "my own had holes." That made him feel better.

"What are you worrying about?" Dillon said, reassuringly. "They look all right to me."

When they were passing the row of water taps with the chained drinking vessels a voice cried, "There's Farrell now." A piece of crust hit Peter on the nose.

"Caesar sends his legate," Dillon murmured. They gathered round. Clancy said, "Hey, boys, Farrell is wearing someone else's boots."

"Who lifted you into them?"

"Wait now," said Clancy, "let's see him walk. Go on—walk Farrell."

Peter backed slowly towards the wall. He backed slowly until he felt the ridge of a downpipe hard against his back. Dillon came with him. "Lay off, Clancy," Dillon said. Swaine was there too. He was smiling, a small cat fat with information.

"Where did you get them, Farrell?"

"Pinched them."

"Found them in an ashbin."

"Make him walk," Clancy insisted, "let's see you walk, Farrell."

"They're my own," Peter said; "they're a bit big—that's all."

"Come on, Farrell—tell us whose they are."

The grins grew wider.

Clancy said, "They're his father's."

"No, they're not," Peter denied quickly.

"Yes, they are. He told Swaine. Didn't he, Swaine? He told you they were his father's."

Swaine's grin froze. Peter fixed him with terrible eyes.

"Well, didn't he, Swaine? Go on, tell the chaps what he told you. Didn't he say they were his father's?"

Swaine edged backwards. "That's right," he said, "he did."

"Hey you chaps," Clancy said, impatiently, "let's make him walk. I vote . . ."

At that moment Peter, with a cry, sprang on Swaine. His fist smashed the glasses on Swaine's face. As they rolled over on the muddy ground, Swaine's nails tore his cheek. Peter saw the white terrified face under him. He beat at it in frenzy until it became covered with mud and blood.

"Cripes," Clancy said in terror, "look at Swaine's glasses. Haul him off lads." They pulled him away and he lashed out at them with feet and hands. He lashed out awkwardly with the big boots which had caused the trouble. Swaine's nose and lips were bleeding so they took him over to the water tap and washed him. Dillon, who stood alone with Peter, brushed his clothes as best he could and fixed his collar and tie.

"You broke his glasses," he said. "There'll be a proper rucky if old Quinny sees him after lunch."

"I don't care about Quinny."

"I do then," Dillon said fervently. "He'll quarter us all in our mother's arms."

They sat with their arms folded while Brother Quinlan in the high chair at the head of the class, gave religious instruction. Swaine kept his bruised face lowered. Without the glasses it had a bald, maimed look, as though his eyebrows, or a nose, or an eye, were missing. They had exchanged no words since the fight. Peter was aware of the boots. They were a defeat, something to be ashamed of. His mother only thought they would keep out the rain. She didn't understand that it would be better to have wet feet. People did not laugh at you because your feet were wet.

Brother Quinlan was speaking of our relationship to one another, of the boy to his neighbour and of the boy to his God. We communicated with one another, he said, by looks, gestures, speech. But these were surface contacts. They conveyed little of what went on in the mind, and nothing at all of the individual soul. Inside us, the greatest and the humblest of us, a whole world was locked. Even if we tried we could convey nothing of that interior world, that life which was nourished, as the poet had said, within the brain. In our interior life we stood without friend or ally—alone. In the darkness and silence of that interior and eternal world the immortal soul and its God were at all times face to face. No one else could peer into another's soul, neither our teacher, nor our father or mother, nor even our best friend. But God saw all. Every stray little thought which moved in that inaccessible world was as plain to Him as if it were thrown across the bright screen of a cinema. That was why we must be as careful to discipline our thoughts as our actions. Custody of the eyes, custody of the ears, but above all else custody. . . .

Brother Quinlan let the sentence trail away and fixed his eyes on Swaine.

"You—boy," he said in a voice which struggled to be patient, "what are you doing with that handkerchief?"

Swaine's nose had started to bleed again. He said nothing. "Stand up boy," Brother Quinlan commanded. He had glasses himself, which he wore during class on the tip of his nose. He was a big man too, and his head was bald in front, which made his large forehead appear even more massive. He stared over the glasses at Swaine.

"Come up here," he said, screwing up his eyes, the fact that something was amiss with Swaine's face dawning gradually on him. Swaine came up to him, looking woebegone, still dabbing his nose with the handkerchief. Brother Quinlan contemplated the battered face for some time. He turned to the class.

"Whose handiwork is this?" he asked quietly. "Stand up, the boy responsible for this."

For a while nobody stirred. There was an uneasy stillness. Poker faces looked at the desks in front of them and waited. Peter looked around and saw Dillon gazing at him hopefully. After an unbearable moment feet shuffled and Peter stood up.

"I am, sir," he said.

Brother Quinlan told Clancy to take Swaine out to the yard to bathe his nose. Then he spoke to the class about violence and what was worse, violence to a boy weaker than oneself.

That was the resort of the bully and the scoundrel—physical violence—The Fist. At this Brother Quinlan held up his large bunched fist so that all might see it. Then with the other hand he indicated the picture of the Sacred Heart. Charity and Forbearance, he said, not vengeance and intolerance, those were qualities most dear to Our Blessed Lord.

"Are you not ashamed of yourself, Farrell? Do you think what you have done is a heroic or a creditable thing?"

"No, sir."

"Then why did you do it, boy?"

Peter made no answer. It was no use making an answer. It was no use saying Swaine had squealed about the boots being his father's. Swaine's face was badly battered. But deep inside him Peter felt battered too. Brother Quinlan couldn't see your soul. He could see Swaine's face, though, when he fixed his glasses on him properly. Brother Quinlan took his silence for defiance.

"A blackguardly affair," he pronounced, "a low, cowardly assault. Hold out your hand."

Peter hesitated. There was a limit. He hadn't meant not to learn the poetry and it wasn't his fault about the boots.

"He's been licked already, sir," Dillon said. "Mr. O'Rourke gave him ten."

"Mr. O'Rourke is a discerning man," said Brother Quinlan, "but he doesn't seem to have given him half enough. Think of the state of that poor boy who has just gone out."

Peter could think of nothing to say. He tried hard but there were no words there. Reluctantly he presented his hand. It was mudstained. Brother Quinlan looked at it with distaste. Then he proceeded to beat hell out of him, and charity and forbearance into him, in the same way as Mr. O'Rourke earlier had hammered in patriotism and respect for Irish History.

It was raining again when he was going home. Usually there were three or four to go home with him, but this afternoon he went alone. He did not want them with him. He passed some shops and walked by the first small suburban gardens, with their sodden gravel paths and dripping gates. On the canal bridge a boy passed him pushing fuel in a pram. His feet were bare. The mud had splashed upwards in thick streaks to his knees. Peter kept his left hand under his coat. There was a blister on the ball of the thumb which ached now like a burn. Brother Quinlan did that. He probably didn't aim to hit the thumb as Mr. O'Rourke always did, but his sight was so bad he had a rotten shot. The boots had got looser than they were earlier. He realised this when he saw Clancy with three or four others passing on the other side of the road. When Clancy waved and called to him, he backed automatically until he felt the parapet against his back.

"Hey Farrell," they called. Then one of them, his head forward, his behind stuck out, began to waddle with grotesque movements up the road. The rest yelled to call Peter's attention. They indicated the mime. Come back if you like, they shouted. Peter waited until they had gone. Then he turned moodily down the bank of the canal. He walked with a stiff ungainly dignity, his mind not yet quite made up. Under the bridge the water was deep and narrow, and a raw wind which moaned in the high arch whipped coldly at his face. It might rain to-morrow and his shoes wouldn't be mended. If his mother thought the boots were all right God knows when his shoes would be mended. After a moment of indecision he took off the boots and dropped them, first one—and then the other —into the water.

There would be hell to pay when he came home without them. But there would be hell to pay anyway when Swaine's father sent around the note to say he had broken young Swaine's glasses. Like the time he broke the Cassidy's window. Half regretfully he stared at the silty water. He could see his father rising from the table to reach for the belt which hung behind the door. The outlook was frightening; but it was better to walk in your bare feet. It was better to walk without shoes and barefooted than to walk without dignity. He took off his stockings and stuffed them into his pocket. His heart sank as he felt the cold wet mud of the path on his bare feet.

THE WEARIN' OF THE GREEN

JOSEPH the Fool did not evolve his idea of planting the suitcase with a time-bomb in it at the Festival Dinner in Murphy's Hotel in the studied and careful manner of the professional conspirator. He was not a conspirator. But to his simple and uncomplicated mind it seemed that the sooner Ballyconlan was free of Murphy, the man of power and property, and Lacey, the Chairman of the Gaelic League, and Father Finnegan, the Parish Priest, together with the lesser lights of the Gaelic League and the Old I.R.A., the better for Ballyconlan, and the better for Ireland at large. There was no difficulty getting the bomb. The bomb was in his possession since the time of the Trouble, when his brother did the difficult jobs and Murphy kept in the background, giving the orders and accepting the credit. It was a heavy and ungainly affair which had been made in the Fitting Shops of the Railway Co. in Dublin and smuggled out with several others for use, first against the British and later against the Irish themselves. Joseph knew how to set the mechanism and had no doubt whatever but that it would work. The suitcase idea had been handed to him readymade in the columns of the *Irish Catholic Times,* where a similar outrage on the clergy of Spain was reported and very much deplored. An Archbiship of Irish descent had died as the result of the injuries he received, so that no known detail of the occurrence had been overlooked. The only thing Joseph lacked was a suitcase. This he obtained from Purcell, the schoolmaster. It was on Purcell's behalf as well as civilization's that he decided to blow the whole bagful up.

Purcell had been kind to him. It was the sort of kindness he had not experienced since his brother had been driven away from Ballyconlan after an innocent but ill-advised attempt to elope with Murphy's daughter. The pair, who throughout the civil war and because of the close contact which had to be maintained between Joseph's brother and Murphy for the successful plotting of various jobs, had been thrown together at odd hours of the day and night and had fallen in love. Despite Murphy's rise to power and wealth and the young fellow's complete unsuitability (he had neither land nor cattle) the attachment continued secretly into more peaceful times. She had been disconsolate and fractious for months after her lover's banishment, but eventually agreed to marry an exenemy of her father, a man who had been on the opposite side during the civil war, but who was now a Town Councillor and a member of the Government. Naturally, Murphy saw no reason against letting bygones be bygones. In public they were bitter enemies; in private, two heads were better than one. It gave him a stake in both camps when eventually his daughter settled down contentedly. The news that Purcell, too, was leaving Ballyconlan at the behest of Murphy did something to the Fool's mind. It gave point and purpose to a confusion of resentments. He suddenly realised why he had kept the bomb by him all the years.

Purcell had taken to the Fool almost immediately on his arrival in Ballyconlan. Tipped-off about the schoolmaster's arrival by Patrick Hennessy, the cabman, Joseph met the newcomer at the station. He was well tipped for the help he gave, which encouraged him to hover near at hand in the ensuing weeks whenever Purcell came into the town for groceries. Purcell, on his part, liked and pitied the Fool. To see him loafing about town—being jeered occasionally by the children because he had a harelip and treated with suspicion by the shopkeepers—touched his always compassionate nature. Joseph seldom shaved, so that although he was mature in years, the hair on his face preserved the downy and untidy quality of adolescence. Purcell thought he looked hungry and hurt. This was not altogether true, for the Fool accepted a multitude of small hospitalities with well-concealed contempt.

"I see you've taken the Fool to the school cottage as a servant," Father Finnegan remarked to Purcell at the beginning.

"I have, Father."

"I don't know that your choice is entirely suitable. In the first place, he's known to be simple-minded."

"I know. I can suffer the little children, Father."

"Can you, Purcell?" (A knitting of the eyebrows.) "He doesn't attend Mass . . . But I suppose you can suffer that, too."

"It's a great pity. But perhaps if people treated you and me as they treat Joseph we too might hesitate about going among them."

"Your compassion does you credit, Purcell. But the real

reason is that my curate condemned that brother of his who tried to seduce the young Murphy one. He said my curate was well paid for it."

Purcell smiled sadly.

"I know," Father Finnegan said; "any of my respected parishioners may say the same thing in a moment of misguided anger. But they would attend Mass." Father Finnegan was large, grey-haired and red-faced. When disciplining his temper he had a habit of stroking his nose with his curled finger, and he did so now. "He may not be completely responsible and possibly does not realise the wrong he does. Nevertheless it gives scandal."

Nevertheless Purcell took the Fool. They lived in the cottage just outside Ballyconlan on a hill from which at night they could see such drab lights as the town boasted. Ballyconlan lay in the valley between two hills. In the course of centuries it had shifted gradually away from the river, which occasionally flooded. In doing so, Ballyconlan jettisoned its last source of occasional excitement. Purcell, wandering from the main street to the railway station on the fringe of the town during the first month of his stay, found that when Murphy's Flour Mills closed, and Murphy's Button Factory ceased work, to the wailing of the same hooter, there was nothing at all for anyone to do except moon around the central square where most of the pubs were located, or play pitch-and-toss at the green patch where the road forked right and left outside the town. Sometimes he followed aimlessly the hypnotic railway line as it climbed the hill to the moorland beyond, a long deserted tract of bog which reflected a lonely and indescribably poignant sky. He dropped into the bar of Murphy's Hotel now and then, where usually there was a commercial traveller to be found, drinking whiskey and making up accounts to fill in the couple of hours to bedtime. It was during this period of adjustment that he decided to start a Choral Society. He played the piano and organ and had produced end-of-term operas as a junior master in Dublin. Through the children in school he succeeded in gathering a sprinkling of adults—sons and daughters of the outlying farmers; and these in turn canvassed their friends among Murphy's factory staff. The rehearsals, at first small impromptu affairs, held in the dilapidated schoolhouse, proved extremely popular. Once a week the young people came along, most of them on bicycles, and eventually, when the rehearsals began to conclude with an impromptu dance, not all who attended were members of the choir. The Choral Society grew almost without Purcell's noticing it, and became the focal point of interest. The young people felt that at last there was something to do in Ballyconlan.

The fact that he had started something of importance was brought home to Purcell when he received his first letter from Lacey, of the Gaelic League, who wrote on behalf of his Committee, protesting against a talk given by Purcell on English Choral Music, while Irish music was being shamefully neglected. The letter filled him with an old weariness. He had not been a school-teacher for some years without several brushes with zealots for the revival of the national language. But he lacked sufficient courage to ignore a letter which could call on the whole weight of the political machine to back it, so he invited Lacey to a rehearsal. He expected a *gauche*, tweed-clad patriot from some Atlantic-stunned parish on the western seaboard. Instead, he was confronted by a precise, bowler-hatted man with a worried expression which a neatly-waxed moustache failed to disguise. He wore a spotless butterfly collar and a dark suit. A gold fáinne decorated his lapel. His waistcoat was dignified by the two symmetrical and massive loops of his watch-chain. He addressed Purcell in Irish, but seemed relieved when he was answered in English. The choir sang some numbers for him, which he gave the impression of hearing with impatient approval.

"A wonderful job, Mr. Purcell," he said, as though appraising a home-made table.

"I'm glad you like it," Purcell said. He rose from the piano and noted, with dismay, that a young man immediately seated himself at it and began vamping a dance number. He tried to lead Lacey out into the grounds, but found a young girl barring his way. She had been in the choir some months before, but after a few sessions had disappeared. Despite his anxiety to get Lacey out of the way, there was something about her which made him forget for a moment the importance of his visitor. Her name hovered in his mind just out of his reach, then came forward pleasurably.

"Sally Maguire," he said, "I thought you had deserted me altogether."

"It wasn't my fault," she said, "it was my father." Her eyes, ignoring Lacey's presence, challenged him with an uncomfortably brazen honesty.

"Has he changed his mind?"

She tilted her head and began to laugh. "I wanted the words of *Drink To Me Only*," she said, avoiding his question. "I wasn't here when you gave them out."

He told her to take a copy from the bundle. His eyes following her involuntarily as she bent over his desk, he noticed the small bruise over her right eye and another on her bare arm. They puzzled him. Meanwhile Lacey was unaware of this distraction.

"It's such a pity the choir is not attached to our Gaelic League Branch," he was saying, in the same rehearsed tone.

"Mr. Murphy would welcome it—heartily. In fact, he told me to tell you so."

"It is very nice of him," Purcell said, "but doesn't he own enough of Ballyconlan already?"

"He's a man of much influence, who could do a lot to help," Lacey observed—rather uneasily, Purcell thought. "He has a wonderful national record."

"Did he kill a lot of people?"

"I expect so. He was in the War of Independence from beginning to end. And self-made, too." Lacey peered around him at the hedges and then ventured a confidence, "as a matter of fact, I can remember him as a gossoon without a seat to his pants." He concluded this with a startling and unexpected titter. The strains of a slow waltz drifting to them from the schoolroom set Purcell wondering irrelevantly if Sally Maguire were dancing with somebody. Lacey's watch-chain, with its pendulant football medals, began to chatter brightly. "The young people of Ireland do not know what men like Mr. Murphy did for them," he continued sadly. "They forget the wrongs of seven hundred years. Listen to that—that foxtrot for instance."

"Yes—a pretty tune, don't you think?"

"But English, Mr. Purcell."

"German. Besides, it's not a foxtrot, it's a waltz."

"Waltz or foxtrot," Lacey said, "it's foreign. That's the danger. These things shouldn't be encouraged. Now, if the choir was attached to our Gaelic League, we could see that only Irish music would be played. It could do a great service in preserving our National Heritage."

"In that case," Purcell said, "you ought organise your own choir."

"We have tried," Lacey answered, "not here in Ballyconlan,

but in other parishes. I'm afraid the young people won't
come." He stared sadly at the dusky, sweet-smelling fields
which were a small part of the Ireland only he and the Gaelic
League knew how to love. Something in the tone of the voice
touched Purcell. His compassion was suddenly aroused for
this sad little man in the butterfly collar. He promised to do
some Moore's melodies in the coming weeks. Lacey seemed
relieved not to have entirely failed in his mission. When Purcell politely refused his final attempt to annex the choir he
shook hands and asked rather sadly why he was so adamant.

"Because," Purcell said, "I think we should cultivate a thing
for itself, not to serve a dubious political aim."

Lacey said regretfully, "You take the narrow view, Mr.
Purcell."

A week later the Fool handed him a letter from the Gaelic
League. Before he opened it, a thought struck Purcell and he
said:

"Do you know Sally Maguire, Joseph?"

"I know the Maguires, Master; there's a tinker's tribe of
them living in the cottage above on Knocknagen Hill."

"This is a girl of about eighteen, a slim dark girl. I noticed
at the rehearsal the other evening she had bruises on her face
and her arm."

"More than like—the father knocks hell out of them when
the humour takes him. She is likely the one who works
in Murphy's button factory."

He had betrayed enough interest in Sally Maguire for the
moment and shifted the conversation.

"Murphy seems to have made plenty of money," he said.
"I wish I knew his secret."

"He didn't make it, Master, he robbed it."

He smiled at this and said, "Was he not put in gaol?"

"No, Master. He's a patriot. During the Trouble it was a fine patriotic thing to hold up a bank or His Majesty's Post Office when the boys were short of funds and lift as much money as you could lay hands on. It was needed to fight the war, but if you put a few hundred in your own pocket to sweeten the risk, it was by way of no harm."

"How do you know all this, Joseph?"

"My brother told me. He did most of the work while Lacey was feathering his nest."

"Joseph," Purcell said, as he opened the letter, "why do they call you the Fool?"

"Because I'm not right in the head, Master," the Fool answered simply.

The letter was from Lacey on behalf of his Committee. Irish music, it declared, suffered more at the hands of gombeen men, like Moore, than through the suppressive activities of the Sassanach himself. The national ideal was to be sought, not in the foreign-dominated drawing-rooms of nineteenth-century Dublin, but in the traditional songs of the people, sung in the people's traditional tongue. It also underlined the responsibility which the official educational programme placed upon Purcell, and hinted at possible representations to Father Finnegan, the school manager. A circular was enclosed with it, inviting him to attend a meeting of the leading townspeople for the purpose of seeking an increase in Old I.R.A. pensions and soliciting his support. The inconsistency did not surprise Purcell in the least.

II

Sally Maguire's attendance at rehearsals created a new interest for Purcell. He had the gallant notion that any man who raised a hand to a woman was a brute, and what he had heard of her distressed him. He resolved to question her about it and decided the best way to make contact was to put her in charge of the music. When she accepted her new office without any fuss or pretension, he found his thoughts more and more preoccupied about her. Despite her rather brazen matter-of-factness she had an elusive charm, a gentleness which intrigued him. Though he did not for a moment think of her as someone he might love (love was not a notion likely to occur to him in any case) he could not regard her dark hair and pale, well-featured face without a new feeling of tenderness. Occasionally he walked some of the road home with her. He found she took as a matter of course the hammerings her father sometimes gave her.

"It was the mother's fault," she confided one night, when he asked about the marks on her arms and her absence from rehearsals. "She was complaining about me going out at night, leaving her to do all the work, and he heard her. He has the divil's temper."

"And he struck you?"

"He knocked hell out of me," she said.

"But your mother should speak to him."

"If she did he'd knock hell out of her too," she returned simply.

"Does he often do that?"

"Not very often. And after a while it's all forgotten. That's how I'm coming to rehearsals again."

During one of their talks he told her of the Gaelic League's opposition, and his decision to put the impromptu social gatherings on a more formal footing. He was going to have a committee appointed and adopt as a name the Ballyconlan Choral Society.

"I'm going to suggest Sweeney as chairman."

"The ex-guard?"

"He used to play in the police band."

"I never liked a polis man," she pronounced sturdily.

"He's all right," Purcell answered. "He has no more love for the Laceys or the Murphys than I have. But I'm wondering what Father Finnegan will have to say."

"He'll try to stop you."

"I feel he will, though I can't see why."

"They hate to see a body enjoying themselves," she answered generally. Purcell was not unused to these over-simplifications. He let it pass.

When he was leaving her she said to him, "People are awful. They love something to gossip about."

"Are they gossiping about the choir?"

"Of course—but I meant about you."

"What about me?"

"About you leaving me home so often."

"Oh . . ." He said no more.

At first Father Finnegan received the proposal with a show of cordiality.

"I'm glad you've come to me, Purcell," he said, offering a chair. "I've had reports of your impromptu—functions."

"Not bad ones, I hope, Father."

A half smile. "Not good ones, I regret to say."

"I'm sorry."

Purcell explained the proposal and gave the names of the Committee.

"I had hoped you were going to ask myself or Father Keenan to act as chairman."

"Unfortunately the members have already made their choice."

"I see. But members should be guided in these matters. I presume you know I expect to be consulted."

"No, Father." As he answered, Purcell realised that that was a lie.

"It seems to me you are not prepared to consult any of us about this society. Is it some sort of undeclared policy not to do so?"

"Not at all, Father. As a matter of fact it started in a very small and informal way. It's because it has developed to such an extent that we got the committee appointed." Father Finnegan had close-cropped grey hair. It showed spikily above saturnine features in which the hue had perceptibly deepened.

"In social activities of any kind it is generally recognised as important to have someone capable of giving spiritual guidance. I am disturbed to learn that the idea does not seem to have occurred to you."

"I'm afraid the importance of spiritual guidance in the simple activity of singing together escaped me, Father."

"Any function where young people of both sexes are thrown together indiscriminately requires supervision. It's not the singing. There will be dances and drinking. I'm thirty years a priest and no fool. Nor are you, Purcell. You know as well as I do what these things lead to. What time do these rehearsals end at?"

"Oh—about 11 o'clock. Seldom later."

"About 11 o'clock. And at that hour young people are to

set off home in one another's company—wandering three or four miles of fields at night time without let or hindrance. You may propose to encourage it. I certainly do not."

"With respect, Father—I can't quite see how having one of the clergy as chairman can alter that. In fact I don't see how my choir meetings can have any bearing on the moral behavior of the young people of the parish—except perhaps to improve it by giving them something to occupy their spare evenings."

"And to give them an excuse for coming together without exciting comment."

"Should they not come together?"

"Under reasonable supervision, yes. That is my province, Purcell."

Purcell realised it was time to make a gesture of capitulation. There were many forces working against him. He saw no reason why they should, but he had been feeling the silent whispering of their small conspiracies for some time.

"If you suggest the safeguards you think necessary, Father," he said, "we will be only too happy to adopt them."

Father Finnegan accepted the surrender without any show of acknowledgment. He would consider the matter and let Purcell know. He had the air of one sufficiently the master of his own power to exercise forbearance.

Shortly afterwards a project to erect a statue in the central square, commemorating the insurgents of 1798, brought Purcell once more into contact with the leading townsfolk. Ballyconlan's connection with the rebellion was not quite clear to him. Everybody at the meeting, however, seemed quite assured about it. Father Finnegan was in the chair. Murphy, in his address, recalled that Ballyconlan had given its sons and daughters in the gallant fight and the blood of these martyrs cried aloud from every green field and every cobbled passage-way for remembrance. In every generation patriots had arisen and it would be a sad day and a misfortunate day the day Ireland forgot them. Murphy, an official patriot himself, spoke with warm conviction. The project itself would be under the auspices of the Gaelic League, but the honour of collecting funds would be everybody's. Purcell's share would be to organise a musical entertainment in the Parish Hall which would feature his choir. After the meeting Murphy unexpectedly offered him a lift.

"Thank you," Purcell said politely, "but I like to walk."

"I wanted a word with you about the choir," Murphy said. "You can count on my help—of course. I'm an influential man—even if I say so myself. A business man—but not a musical one. Too hard a life, I suppose. . . ."

Purcell smiled at the implication.

"It's very kind of you," he said, "but I feel we can manage on our own."

"Two heads, Purcell," the other said, "—better than one. You do the music, but who will handle the business?"

"The committee—in their own fashion, which is best."

"Business is business. I can do a lot to help. In fact I've wanted to talk to you for a long time, Purcell. The Choral Society can help me—a fair arrangement. I like to play an active part in any of the town's social activities."

Purcell saw that only a direct refusal would be taken as an answer. He summoned his will to give it, knowing that he was going to make an influential enemy. He saw quite clearly that this was a moment of crisis.

"You are a public man, Mr. Murphy," he said, "and I appreciate your interest. But I am a schoolmaster, and what little I have learned from my experience convinces me that there is only one way to help our people. They must be allowed to develop of themselves. They must learn, however dangerously, to run their own affairs. . . ."

"You mean you won't tolerate interference."

"Not at all. I mean to make the unpopular experiment of helping them to grow something their own way."

III

Purcell, poised on the stepladder with his hand outstretched to open the schoolroom window, heard the rattle of teacups and looked down at the gathering. Tea after rehearsals was one of the first innovations of the ladies on the committee. It invested the proceedings with an air of respectability sufficiently slight to increase rather than diminish enthusiasm. Sally Maguire was collecting music and putting it on his desk; a group of youths had gathered about the piano while another tried his hand at a popular tune; cigarette smoke in tapering ascent clouded about the naked electric bulbs. There was a warm odour from the tea urn which bubbled its friendly conversation in the far corner. These meetings of the choral society, these hands passing around tea and biscuits, the self-conscious badinage, even the occasional horseplay, had become very dear to him, the more so since he had seen its spontaneity threatened. Father Finnegan had cocked a nose to the wind and scented licence; Murphy recognised in it a new social unit and wanted it because he saw all such units as potentially political. The Gaelic League, having failed to impose its concept of music as an affair comprising kilts and bagpipes, sought to kill it. The crozier and the hurling stick were raised in menace. He opened the window and the cool autumn-smelling air made him suddenly aware of hushed, harvest-shorn fields, and winding laneways where leaves in odd unexpected movement surprised the darkness. It recalled for him the fact that besides announcing the opera which the committee on his advice had decided to undertake, he was also to arrange to operate Father Finnegan's suggestion for putting the moral side of things right. These dark fields with their harvest-heavy breath were dangerous. The girls and men were to go home after rehearsals in groups and not to go in mixed couples. As he got down from the ladder he realised that the actual announcement was going to cause him embarrassment. He went to the middle of the floor and clapped his hands. He tried always to forget he was a schoolteacher but there were occasional little mannerisms which betrayed him. When there was silence he cleared his throat.

"Before we continue, there's something I have to say. As you know we have been asked to give our support to the '98 Fund collection and your committee have agreed to produce a show in the Town Hall late in November. The decision is to produce *The Pirates of Penzance*, an opera with delightful music which I know you will enjoy rehearsing. The details are to be worked out later, but I can assure you here and now that you will find it much more difficult than anything we have attempted heretofore. It will mean more frequent and longer rehearsals. And that brings me to a communication which I received from Father Finnegan and which I propose to read to you." When he had finished the letter he went over to Sweeney the chairman, who assured him the suggested arrangement would be carried out. No girl would go home alone in the company of a member of the opposite sex. There was a good deal of giggling over it. Purcell felt it provoked a new intimacy between the younger people by being too frankly suspicious. He had a feeling it would not be carried out. In the meanwhile he had his own problem. It affected his own walks with Sally Maguire which, without bothering to consider why, he had grown to enjoy so much. Now he asked Sweeney to come some of the way with them.

"Do you think I'm a bloody chaperon?" Sweeney asked.

"I can't give bad example."

"For the love of God, man—show a bit of sense."

"I am. Plenty of people in Ballyconlan would welcome the opportunity of pointing out to Father Finnegan that the schoolmaster was not treating his wishes with respect."

"But you're a grown and responsible man."

"For the sake of the society I don't mind being treated like a little boy."

So Sweeney, to Sally Maguire's obvious resentment, began to come home with them.

One night a month later he was losing heart and said to Sweeney: "Everything is going very well on the singing side, but I'm worried about expenses. These costumes are going to cost a lot to hire; the royalties are heavy. Maybe I should get Murphy's backing after all."

"No," Sweeney said, "keep that crowd out."

"What are we to do?"

"We'll pay for our own and have a subscription to help those who can't."

"Another matter," Purcell said. "I have a letter from the Gaelic League."

"Lacey?"

"Lacey signs it—but I expect Murphy is behind it. They object to the *Pirates* as a Sassanach production, likely to corrupt our Irish heritage."

"The seven hundred years."

"Precisely. But calling it that doesn't answer the letter. What am I to say?"

"Tell him to go to hell."

"I'm tired telling people to go to hell. I'm tired standing on my own. Isn't it time I got some help?"

"Then put it to the Committee and *we'll* tell him. After all, rehearsals have gone too far now to start chopping and changing. I suppose they still want Irish airs."

"They say they would be more appropriate to a Ninety-Eight Concert."

"I know what they want," Sweeney said with feeling, "bits and scraps of things with neither taste nor smell about them. I went through it all I can tell you."

The Committee agreed. They were going to do the opera. Apart from a general restiveness, an impatience with the traditional restrictions, they were keenly interested in the music. Besides, anticipation of footlights, colourful costumes and the long days of occupation and interest which promised ahead strengthened them. So they informed the League that rehearsals were too far advanced for any change to be practicable.

Another night as they walked home together Purcell said to Sally Maguire: "Sweeney is going down into town on some business. You'll have to trust me alone."

"Am I supposed to weep?"

Her tone surprised him.

"I'm referring to Father Finnegan's stipulations . . ."

"Father Finnegan doesn't have to worry."

He smiled. "You can look after yourself."

"Good God, no."

He puzzled for some time. Then he said, "I don't follow."

Her laugh answered him from the darkness.

"You're a bloody slow one." He was mildly alarmed.

Meanwhile nothing further came from the Ninety-Eight Fund Committee. Various functions were held, including a football match which, though attended to capacity, yielded surprisingly little in cash (Ballyconlan exhibiting the traditional reluctance to pass through an official entrance when it could slip in over the fence); a Sale of Work in the Town Hall which did better; a Gaelic League Dance; a Whist Drive, which failed miserably because no one in Ballyconlan played whist. At last, Purcell wrote asking for assistance and after four weeks received a reply. The Ninety-Eight Committee did not consider the proposed performance suitable. As an alternative, a drama group from Dublin had been engaged to give performances in the town on the dates in question. It was an amateur group of proved ability and excellent national character.

He was unprepared for the anger with which the Committee received the announcement. "They're not going to get away with it," one of them said. The remark became a sort of standard about which they rallied. Hope of doing something really important had been raised too high to be crushed out so suddenly. In the past few weeks something unheard of and undreamt of in Ballyconlan had been shown to be eminently possible. With unusual disregard for good money they decided to pay for the entire production themselves by saving over a period of months. It meant postponing the performance, but since it no longer had any connection with the Ninety-Eight Fund that did not matter. They agreed, tentatively, to aim at performances during the first and second week in the following July. When, after Christmas, it was announced that the statue would be unveiled during the first week of July, they fixed the time definitely. There would be people in town and the air of carnival would assure good attendances.

Naturally, word of their intentions got around. Opinion among those outside the society, at first divided, gradually, if secretly, hardened in favour of the Choral Society. Nobody cared much for Murphy, if for no other reason than that he was powerful. Gossip soon reduced it to a fundamental issue; the Schoolmaster against Murphy. People thought him a foolish young man, but liked him for it. The fact that the Parish Priest and the Gaelic League favoured Murphy was only to be expected. Power coalesced. It was circulated that it was an immoral opera and that Father Finnegan was going to kick up holy murder about it from the pulpit. Yet Sunday followed Sunday and Father Finnegan was silent. Near the end of May, Purcell was told by Sally Maguire of the first positive move.

"Murphy is putting us on overtime at the factory," she said. "It's all over the place."

Purcell was unperturbed.

"He's left it a bit late. It will make things difficult, but not impossible."

"Whatever he does, I'm coming to rehearsals. I don't care what happens."

"I wish everybody had your spirit, Sally," he said warmly. She looked at him quickly. But he was still platonic, the good father, the big brother.

He went to Father Finnegan.

"There's some talk that you consider the opera immoral, Father. I've brought you a copy of the script."

"I've already examined the script, Purcell," Father Finne-gan said.

"Do you consider it immoral?"

"Personally, no. but a moral judgment is a difficult one to make. My parishioners think it immoral. It could be argued, therefore, that it is."

"How in God's name does that follow?"

"If it offends their sense of morality . . ."

"Your parishioners know nothing at all about it. They've never read the script. Most of them never heard of Gilbert and Sullivan. They are being told it's immoral and that you con-sider it so."

"I am doubtful about the character of Ruth. A lone woman with a band of pirates—to some of my parishioners the impli-cations will be obvious."

"What of the character of the schoolmaster who selected it? There are implications there, too."

Father Finnegan looked directly at Purcell and saw that he was sincere. He turned away.

"In point of fact," he said, "I do not consider the script im-moral." Then, as an afterthought, he added:

"While you're here, there is another matter I should like to mention to you. I am informed that you have been keeping company with the young Maguire girl."

"What is the ugly implication this time?"

The tone of goaded antagonism made Father Finnegan raise his eyebrows.

"I do not believe there is any ugly implication. There is gos-sip."

"The gossip is malicious. I know where it emanates from."

Father Finnegan's voice altered. "I'm no fool, Purcell," he said; "I've told you so before; and I can assure you that I will deal uncompromisingly with slander—whatever source it may spring from. It is only that I feel you should be warned. You are not any Tom, Dick or Harry here. You are the school-master. That makes all the difference. And you are becoming bitter, against the institutions of the community, and against me. You are hardening your heart. That is dangerous."

It was the first human thing that had passed between them in their interviews. The fact that the initiative should come from the priest affected Purcell.

His mood quietened. "You're wrong about the bitterness, Father. I have my own way of looking at things, which I do not think is in conflict either with the Church or society. I've done no wrong."

"That's what the Pharisee said."

"In righteousness. I plead it in defence—not positively, but negatively."

"I don't doubt your motives for a moment," Father Finne-gan said. Then he smiled. "If I did, I'd declare myself openly." Purcell smiled too.

"Please God that won't be necessary, Father."

"Please God it won't."

They had established contact with one another, a mutual respect, which heartened Purcell considerably. For the first time in many months he saw some hope of success.

IV

Purcell checked his list of characters as Sweeney opened the boxes and examined the costumes which had arrived. There was an air of suppressed excitement in the schoolroom. Some of the cast were present, and the inevitable amateur was already seated at the piano, vamping a discordant bass to a popular tune. But those who worked in the factory had been kept back after tea on special work. Three or four rehearsals recently had been spoiled by these sudden decisions of the factory management. Purcell had advised them to work when they were instructed to do so. He was terrified of dismissals and consequent trouble. To-night, however, Sweeney reported that they intended to walk out at eight o'clock.

"Is there no way to stop them?" Purcell had asked.

"A lot of irresponsible young ones—you know what they are when they get an idea into their heads," Sweeney answered. "I hope to God I don't lose my pension on the head of them."

"Flag—Pirate Chief," Purcell said, absently ticking the item with his pencil. "I think that's practically everything, except the orchestra parts. What did you order?"

At a quarter past eight most of those from the factory arrived. They had walked out. Purcell thought it a mistake and said so to Sweeney. "There'll be bloody murder," Sweeney said. "I'll bet it's all over town already."

But there was no use saying anything about it to them. Besides, he caught something of their excitement and felt the spirit of their revolt affecting him personally, as they undid parcels and changed into costumes. There was some horseplay and it was difficult at first to marshal them for the opening chorus. The rehearsal was hard to control, but it went very well. It finished near midnight.

When it was over, he remarked happily to Sweeney that nothing could stop the show from going on the following week.

"What about the costumes?" he asked, looking around at the

disorderly schoolroom where boxes and baskets lay scattered with clothes straggling untidily from them.

"It's very late," Sweeney insisted; "leave it all to me. You get some rest."

He walked with Sally Maguire up the hill from the school-house. The sultry darkness was quiet about them, the wind soothing after so much excitement.

"Thank God Sweeney isn't with us," she said.

"You don't like Sweeney. I can't see why."

"I don't mind Sweeney at all. I—I just don't want him with us to-night."

Something in her tone excited him. He was suddenly conscious of her proximity and their aloneness together under a brown blanket of sky, and the warm wind on their faces which smelled of fields and flowers. Tenderly he said:

"Sally—won't you get into a hell of a row about what happened to-night?"

"We'd do more than that," she said offhandedly. "Don't you realise what it means to us—the Choral Society and the bit of gaiety there is since you started it?" She shook his arm. "There was no life at all before it, not a thing from one end of the week to another. You came along and stood up to Murphy and his set. You were not afraid of Father Finnegan and the quality. There's something to look forward to now which they can't get their hands on and spoil. We couldn't let them stop us now."

"I can't understand why they didn't start anything themselves. Was there nothing in the factory?"

"Nothing at all—except some of the boys annoying you going home."

He said gallantly, "That's the penalty you pay for being pretty."

"Do you think I'm pretty?" she asked him openly.

"Of course I do," he answered. He felt the subtle change which the remark made in their relationship and attempted a noncommital note by adding: "The Ballyconlan Society is going to be noted for its pretty chorus." He realised immediately that he had said the wrong thing, but they walked for about ten minutes in silence before her arm left his as they came to a standstill. She went over towards the stile which led to the path through the woods, a short cut for her, but one they never used. She said good-bye to him, over her shoulder, with the minimum of ceremony.

"I'm taking the short cut," she said. "It's very late."

"You'll be mud up to the eyes," he joked, calling it after her, but she didn't answer. He hesitated. Then her sudden exclamation and the sound of her stumbling made him call her name. Impulsively he made for the stile. The silence under the tall trees on the far side alarmed him and when there was no answer he began to grope in the darkness with his hands. "Sally," he called again and again. "Where are you—Sally?" until a voice, almost at his ear, said softly, "I'm here."

"My God," he questioned, "are you hurt?" He bent down over her, discerning first the white outline of her face and then her slim form stretched out beside him. He put his arm about her shoulders. She tilted her face.

"Would you like to kiss me?" she asked blandly. For a moment he was angry. Then a sickly sweat of desire surged through him. He found her lips and for a long time he was unaware of anything except their moist softness. When at last he released her it was she who rose first. Without a word she began to run down the path. "Sally," he called, but softly this time, the passion she had roused, though controlled once more, still unabated. Her good-night came back softly to him between the leaf-whispering trees.

Two hours later he was in bed but still awake, listening to the rain which beat incessantly on the roof of the cottage, when the knocking on the door startled him. The kitchen was fire-lit and warm as he crossed it to unbolt the door. The rain blinded him for a moment, but then he recognised her and his heart almost stopped beating.

"Sally," he said, "what has happened?"

He moved his own clothes, which Joseph had lit the fire to dry, and sat her down. The lamplight revealed a bruise on her cheek. She told him there had been a row when she got home over the walk-out at the factory. Her father had been waiting up for her. He had seen the mud of the ditch on her coat and come to the conclusion which Purcell, despite his rage, could not condemn as unjustifiable.

"He knocked hell out of me, and when I hit back at him he threw me out," she said. Then, as though in answer to a question, she added, "Who else could I go to?"

He roused Joseph, who took in the situation without any show of surprise. Over supper it was arranged she should have his bed, and in the morning he would find ways and means of getting her away. She wanted to go to Dublin. The decision she had taken, her long journey back through the rain, seemed to have exhausted her, so that she listened to him meekly and submitted almost without interest to all he said. Long after she had retired he lay awake on the makeshift bed which he had set up in Joseph's room. It was the most dangerous situation he had ever been in in his life and yet it was not that which occupied him chiefly. He found his thoughts straying again and again to the fact that she who had tried blatantly some few hours previously to seduce him was now only a few feet from him in the darkness of the next room. Now it was he who was full of uneasiness and she who was passive, and, for the moment anyway, at rest. He recalled the sound of her voice, her pale face, the mockery which could light so quickly and so attractively in her eyes. He left her sleeping. But he slept very little himself.

The next day the postman saw her. He came up the hill at an unusual hour with a heavy parcel which Purcell found lying on the table for him when he returned from the village. The parcel had English stamps on it and was registered. She and Joseph were upset at their mistake, but Purcell, after the first shock of it, accepted the situation like a man who had known that this must inevitably happen sooner or later. Victory had been coming too easily. He knew exactly how events would develop when tongues started to wag, as they would, almost immediately, and her father went to Father Finnegan to have him accused. His main concern was to get her away quickly and safely, which he succeeded in doing when the car he had engaged arrived early the following morning. There was a light veil of mist still crowning the wooded slopes of the hill and, as he said goodbye to her, he was aware of the peace which surrounded him, the sunlight on the lower fields and the birds testing the sweet-smelling air of morning. He would have liked to kiss her in token of what little existed between them, but the presence of Joseph and the driver of the car restrained him. Instead, he pressed her hand and told her to write to him, a request which he knew to be stupid and pointless when, later that evening, after a day spent in fruitless examination of the situation in which he was involved, Father Finnegan's letter arrived. It was as he expected. The priest appeared to be under the impression that she was still in the cottage, because he commanded him under God's Law to pack her back to her parents at once, and to attend at the priest's house in the morning for an interview, at which Father Finnegan would do his painful duty in response to the demands of the leading people of the town and with the blessing of every decent father and mother in Ballyconlan.

Purcell left the letter down and picked up the parcel which had started the talk. It contained the four or five band parts for the opera.

"Joseph," he said, "I want you to bring this to the post office first thing to-morrow to be returned to the sender. And when you come back I want to start packing. I'm leaving to-morrow evening."

"Leaving, master?"

"Leaving, Joseph. What else is there to do? Every decent father and mother in Ballyconlan wants me to. So do the leading townsfolk."

"But you did no harm."

"I did, Joseph. I didn't mean to. It seemed the most natural thing in the world to me to start a society which would keep the boys and girls of the parish amused. But I forgot the important people; the patriots and the priests, who must test everything first to assure themselves that the plan is set out on Irish-made paper which has been watermarked with the Sixth Commandment. Murphy, for instance, has a corner in patriotism. He sincerely believes that our forefathers wore kilts and played Gaelic football when they weren't writing Aislings. He has taken some pains to know about such things. What is to happen to him and his henchmen if there is a swing in favour of *opera buffa* and cricket? That would constitute a betrayal of the national ideal, because Murphy is himself the National Ideal. Father Finnegan thinks he can make the marriage rate compatible with the birth rate by beating courting couples out of the national ditch with the walking stick of morality. To argue with him at all is to attack the Catholic Church, because Father Finnegan is the be-all and end-all of Catholicism. Every priest his own pope. And, fundamentally, the couples have no belief in either of them, as their conduct when they get to hell out of the country, as I intend to do, amply proves. If the Gaelic League really want to sell the national ideal to the young people in the ditches, I could give them a slogan: Kilts are more Convenient. But Father Finnegan would object."

He paused and smiled, because he had been talking for the sake of talking. In his heart he was deeply wounded at the unexpected turn of events.

"Light the lamps, Joseph, it's getting dark," he said.

Joseph began the nightly operation for the last time. In the darkening kitchen he pumped the kerosene lamp until its buzzing took on the sleepy familiarity of every night and became an unnoted background to their thoughts.

"I'll leave with you, master," he answered. The plan was already in his mind. It had come to him quite easily and naturally as he pumped at the lamp. It filled him with peace. He stood against the background of his own colossal shadow, which filled the wall behind him, his eyes fixed in contemplation of his plan, his huge harelip slung like a drinking trough from his face.

"But where would you go?"

"I would go to a person I know—for a while. If I had a suitcase that would take my few things."

"You can have one of mine."

"Which one, master?"

"Whatever one you fancy. One is as bad as the other. It's good we both travel light, Joseph."

"To-morrow I won't travel light, master."

Purcell dismissed it as one of the unaccountable things the Fool often said. But when he had gone to bed Joseph made himself busy. He fetched the bomb from its hiding-place and took its parts asunder, staring at them until slowly the procedure of long years ago came back to him, the routine of those far-off nights when he sat up to help his brother, who fought to establish a new Ireland by blowing hell out of the British Empire. Then he fetched out the three cases and, deciding that the faded green one with the unaccountable initials C. D. stencilled on it was the most suitable for his purpose, made it ready. The next morning, while he was bringing the three cases to Patrick Hennessy, who waited at the foot of the hill with his scrawny horse and ramshackle cab, he set the mechanism carefully for ten o'clock. He reckoned they would all be in the hotel by then.

"These two," he explained carefully to Hennessy, "is the master's. They're to be left in the waiting-room below at the station."

"Right," Hennessy said.

"And this one," he said, "if you'll do a little turn for me . . ."

"Of course," said Hennessy.

". . . you might leave at the hotel on your way down."

"Is it one of the quality's?"

"It is . . . a Dublin gentleman that's going to dinner to-night. It's to be left in the corner of the dining-room, beside the piano, so that he can find it."

Hennessy, who was wise about entertainments, said:

"I expect he's one of them conjurers."

"That's right," Joseph said, "he's a conjurer. I carried it down for him early this morning."

"Dammit, but you were quick enough getting back into business again, Joseph."

"I was."

Hennessy leaned over confidentially.

"Tell me this—about your man above . . ."

"What man?"

"Now, now—what man? The schoolmaster. Tell me this."

"Not now. I'll tell you it all to-night after the train comes. But you'll be careful to do what I've told you about the case there."

"I'll do that—don't fret. Did you see them unveiling the statue this morning? I'll declare to God but it brought plenty to the town."

"It should have kept them away from the town," Joseph said violently.

Patrick Hennessy frowned down at him.

"You're a contrairy bloody man," he observed in a puzzled tone, before flicking his whip.

V

The statue, the man, stood newly carved in stone, his pike tilted in slim menace at the unbelligerent houses opposite, where some children played marbles in the gutter and a dog with vigorous enjoyment scratched its mongrel belly. Purcell paused to look at it for a moment. Hoary Michael Hannigan was sitting on the seat near the statue, the only other adult in the square, sucking comfort from his clay pipe in the warm waning of the July evening. In all the streets converging on the square, rows and rows of bunting dissected the sky into ragged drills. Purcell walked alone under the small flags which flaunted their triangular colours, and banners which blazed with slogans. Remember '98. A Nation Once Again. God Bless Our Pope. Warm odours drifting from the open window's of Murphy's Hotel informed him of the preparations for the festive dinner. From the distant fairground an amplifier pumped out patriotic music. It merely emphasised the loneliness of the hour and the loneliness of his own journey to the station on this evening, which was to have seen the presentation of the opera, his final triumph. Nobody had come to see him off. Even Joseph had disappeared without a word of farewell. As he moved out of the square to waste the hour which was left before it was time to catch his train, he felt that most of all. He found the lanes about the station deserted too, and full of the indifferent tranquillity of the evening. Lying back against a green bank, conscious of the drowsy meadowland, the hum of insects, the faint odours of cattle which hung about the lane, he lit a cigarette and began to go over it all in his mind, feeling like a Lear deserted even by his Fool.

Patrick Hennessy climbed down from his cab with the caution of his age and came over without a word to join Hoary Michael Hannigan. They surveyed the statue in mutual silence.

"That's a commendable piece of stonework," Hannigan volunteered at last. He was leaning forward on his stick, his grey hair falling untidily about the back of his upturned head.

"What does it say on the pedestal there?" Hennessy asked.

He had had a good day's business, with plenty of free whiskey to keep him away from melancholy.

"Damn the bit of me knows," Hannigan said. "It's all in Irish."

"Nor Murphy either, for all his cáirde gaels when he was unveiling it."

"Wait now," said Hannigan, who had moved around the side and was peering forward to counteract the slow waning of the long day's light, "it's in English here."

He began to read.

> *Erected By the People of Ballyconlan, to the*
> *Memory of the Men of The Insurrection Who*
> *in 1798 Fought and Died for Irish Freedom.*
>
> *By red wave of Slaney and Barrow they fell*
> *The tyrannous Saxon to conquer and quell.*

"They were fine men. You won't see the likes of them today."

"I wouldn't mind," Hennessy said, "but the get-up of a bloody gombeen man who unveiled it."

"There he is now—getting out of his car with Lacey of the Gaelic League."

"I can't see that far," Hennessy complained. "I suppose he's wearing his 1916 medal."

"The pair of them," Hannigan reported; "they'd catch cold if they went out without them."

"I wouldn't mind—but it's highly debatable if Murphy or Lacey ever got within earshot of a gun."

"They have their fine fat pensions for it, anyway," said Hennessy, "and their seats on the County Council."

The two old men watched the cars of the new social hierarchy arrive. Father Finnegan came next. He was joined by
the doctor. Murphy shook hands with both of them and, as
they ascended the steps, the committee members of the Gaelic
League, who were speaking in Irish to one another, gave passage. Joseph the Fool came through the Square and Hannigan
called him. He stared at them with wide expressionless eyes,
his closely cropped head a little to one side, his undeveloped
body ungainly. The sleeves of his coat were so short that half of
each forearm protruded nakedly.

"Are you not joining the quality?" Hannigan twitted him.
Joseph ignored him and questioned Hennessy.

"You left the case in as I said?"

"I did that," Hennessy said, "in the corner by the piano."

"Are you sure?"

"I ought to be—I'm in and out and up and down that
bloody stairs all evening. And very little to show for it—mind
you."

Hannigan chuckled and interrupted him. "I saw the schoolmaster passing a while back. You'd wonder he had the neck
after the carry-on of him with Sally Maguire."

Joseph narrowed his eyes.

"He did no harm," he said.

"I have it different, then," Hannigan answered.

"He did her no harm," the Fool insisted, "only the harm he
did himself. He gave her his bed when her own father threw
her out, and when she was hungry he put the bit of food in her
belly."

"He put more than food in it," chuckled Hennessy, "if ru-
mour has it right." Then, as an afterthought, he added, "God
forgive me."

The hoot of an engine silenced the laughter of the old men. The Fool looked at the statue as though, while they were talking, it had sprouted silently from the ground.

"That man with the pike has blind eyes," he said—startling them.

After a while, the old men left. Hennessy had money in his pocket which he invited Hannigan to help him spend. But Joseph sat on. He kept vigil with his elbows resting on his knees, his fists clenched under his chin. A burst of applause which overflowed into the square greeted Father Finnegan as he rose to begin the speechmaking. Everybody's thanks were due to Mr. Murphy, the President of the '98 Fund Committee (he said), a man who was a credit, a very great credit indeed, to the town of Ballyconlan. Murphy's Hotel, he would say, without fear of contradiction, was one of the best in Ireland, and his factory one of the most modern, for although we protected with jealous pride the traditional culture of our people, we were prepared, and rightly prepared, to examine and take to ourselves what was the worthy result of progress in other nations, whose history—happier than ours—had allowed them to develop their industrial processes to a higher pitch of efficiency. He must not forget to thank ex-Guard Sweeney, either, who presided so gracefully at the piano. Here was a confluence of sweet sounds to charm the ears of all, and to fill the heart with the proud knowledge that our native music could compare more than favourably with the best in the world. What could be more lovely than our Irish songs and dances? Of course, there were Irishmen,—God help them (laughter)— who were prepared to ape the English taste for comic operas —and what could that be, after all, but a heathen taste; and others, of course, who wanted nothing less than Bach and Beethoven—he would refer to these gentlemen as the long-haired militia (laughter)—and who decried our native music for being too unsophisticated for their discriminating palates. But so far as he, personally, was concerned, and he was sure all present would agree with him, give him the good old Irish tunes every time. Give him these and he wouldn't give that (snap of the fingers) for all the symphonies and high falutin concertos of the Big Wigs.

So Father Finnegan went on, proposing the toast of Ireland, while the evening tarried above the town, and the fields of Ireland, which the blood of patriots had fertilised over long and painful centuries, lay passively and awaited its coming. Joseph sat so still that the old mongrel, forgetting the distrust of long experience, came and laid its muzzle on his knee. Joseph felt the warmth for some time before he pushed it away. It ambled for diversion over to the statue, a new amenity, and pissed wearily against its base. Hiss-piss-hiss sang its slaney-green wave from under a piky foot. Then it left Joseph to watch alone.

Purcell, who had the carriage to himself, watched the slow fading of the evening, too. It brought Sally Maguire to his mind. He wondered whether he should try to find her to-morrow or whether to let the whole business die. He would write to Father Finnegan, of course, and tell him what had occurred. After that there would be time to make up his mind; he had the long summer vacation in which to do so. He might go to England or, perhaps, further afield. Looking at his watch he found it was five minutes to ten. That gave him something over an hour before he would reach Dublin. He pulled one of the travelling cases, which the porter had left on the seat beside him, and lay it on the floor, wondering for a moment at its weight. It was the faded green one, with the unaccountable initials, C. D., stencilled on it. Stretching out his legs to rest his heels on it, he lay back. The train was travelling bogland once again, a brown and lonely expanse, dotted with poignant pools, in which the last light of the evening lingered and was drowned.

THE DAMNED

HIS mother's hand shook his shoulder. When he opened his eyes she had the still-tall Christmas candle lighting on the dressing table. It was the Christmas candle lighting but Christmas was three months ago. Its yellow unsteady light made him screw up his eyes. A solitary bell was ringing somewhere outside, somewhere far off across a space of cold, early-morning darkness. The blankets were lovely and soft and warm, but his nose was cold.

Six o'clock, his mother said.

Warm dreamless sleep he longed to sink deep down back into but his mother's hand kept dragging him up from its fluffy depths, and his eye opened, closed, opened like the cat's when she dozed at the fire. When at last they stayed open she said again six o'clock son and he could see she was smiling at him. She had a long nightdress on her and a shawl about her shoulders. All her face looked very old and tired and she had her teeth out. It frightened him to see her face worn and tired bending over him in candlelight and her teeth out. She was like dead and he would pray for her at Mass.

As he washed he made sure not to swallow any water because he was going to receive Holy Communion. His good suit was laid out for him and his shoes were polished.

Joe and Aunt Mary were here last night, his mother told him, they brought you a new shirt.

He murmured sleepily.

Aunt Mary is as good as gold, she added. He knew from her voice she was near to tears. Whenever she mentioned a kindness now it moved her to tears. Aunt Mary, her sister, had a habit lately of bringing little gifts. Since his father's death she would call and say: How are you Ellen, in a warm voice. His mother said: Keeping the best side out. What else is a body to do. And once when he was there, pretending not to mind, his mother said: I'm worried about who-you-know. He's fretting. Who-you-know was him. Aunt Mary said: He saw it happen, the poor child. Is he still . . . I mean at night? He pulled on the shirt, which smelled nice and new.

His feet rang emptily on the path. Sometimes from a faraway street he heard feet as early as his own give answer; and now three different bells were ringing. The street lamps were on, which made it look like night, but the darkness was cold and more lonely than night darkness. From around corners a small sharp wind made ambush now and then and in the unswept gutters pieces of paper flurried and scraped. He passed the graveyard of the Protestant Cathedral. Once it belonged to the Catholics but the Protestants took it. They desecrated the Altar and the holy vessels. They would burn forever in hell for that. He glanced fearfully through the railings at the leaning headstones and thought of their blackened tormented faces howling through the flames and their screaming, struggling nakedness and then he thought of himself, his soul pure and white, hurrying through the dark, windy, early morning streets to serve Mass and receive the Immaculate Host which was God Incarnate, the Unsuffering Victim, and he shuddered. Last night in confession he had told Father Rogan he prayed for the damned and Father Rogan said no, he must not do so. As he looked at the headstones a piece of white paper whirled past him with startling suddenness. The wind pinned it against the railings. It flapped and struggled. Then it went whirling and spinning again into the darkness among the tombstones, lost and helpless, pursued by the wind. He hurried on, frightened.

He put on his soutane and surplice and went into the vestry. Father Rogan, who was robed and reading his prayers silently, looked around at him. To avoid meeting his eyes, he pretended to see if the cruets were filled. Then he took a taper and went out to light the altar candles. There were six tall ones at the back and a small one on each side of the tabernacle. When he turned, Father Rogan was ready. "Are you receiving—John?" he asked. "Yes, Father," he said. It was only a formality because Father Rogan knew. In confession he had promised Father Rogan to offer his Communion for the repose of his father's soul. The thought of his father troubled him for a moment as he preceded the priest on to the altar, but the holy things around him made him feel less afraid.

During Mass it grew very warm on the altar and the Latin came in low somnolent murmurs, so that he had to strain forward to know where to make the responses. Father Rogan's face became absorbed and pole and his eyelids drooped heavily. Sometimes he gave a great sigh. When a member of the congregation came in late you heard first of all the soft tread of feet and then the clap of padded doors, and quite a while later the candle flames wavered and danced and sent up little plumes of smoke. Then they stood still again, each tipped by its golden flame which burned like a pure soul. But if one blew out it was smoky and black, like a damned soul. Father Rogan looked at him very intently when he turned and said *Orate Fratres,* but he knew he was not thinking of him at all. Father Rogan had been very angry with him in confession last night when he said he had prayed for the damned again. But now he had promised not to do it any more. Father Rogan had said the Damned hated God because God said to them, "Depart from me ye cursed into everlasting flames which were prepared for the Devil and his angels." It was useless to pray for these wicked souls who mocked at God's beauty and spat blasphemies in His face. It was dark and cold in the confession box and outside he had heard the clerk's keys rattling while he locked up the church. Then he forgot the cold and the keys and he thought only of God and heaven and hell.

Are many souls damned, father? he had asked.

Father Rogan had breathed heavily and shifted and said a little wearily: You think a lot about hell?

Did he think a lot about it now? Yes, he thought a lot about it, but he tried not to. When he prayed for his father he thought about it.

I dream often about hell, Father.

What do you dream?

About flames and black faces and being lost. He hesitated. One of the black faces he always knew.

There is something else, Father Rogan suggested.

I think of God, Father, when I wake up.

In what way?

The sweat broke out coldly about his eyes, but hot and moist where his shirt clung to his stomach.

Father . . . he attempted. His tongue with shame and blasphemy filled his mouth like a sausage.

Don't be ashamed, child, Father Rogan helped gently, you are not telling me—you are telling God. It was even harder to tell God, though God knew already.

I see God without any clothes on.

Is it an obscene image?

I—I think so, Father.

Do you entertain it . . . dwell on it?

Oh, no, Father, he said. His fervour satisfied the priest.

That's right, Father Rogan assured him, you must put it out of your mind. But don't worry or feel ashamed. The devil conjures up these evil visions to tempt and frighten you. Even the saints, very great and holy men, have complained of this.

I see, Father, he said. Then, without meaning to, he found himself saying again:

But are many souls damned, Father?

Father Rogan had hesitated. Then in an almost brutal tone he said: The Little Flower tells us that in one of her visions she saw souls falling into hell like leaves from the trees.

There was silence.

And Our Blessed Lady made known to us that more souls are lost through the sin of impurity than through all the other sins put together.

More silence. The priest had waited and after a time leaned towards the grill.

Now, my child, the priest said very gently, you must try to tell me what is really troubling you.

Yes, Father, he said. Then a tear trickled down his nose and fell on his hand. The priest waited. He began to sob. He could not help now but to cast away all evasion and lay naked his heart.

Father, he said, I think my Daddy is in hell.

Father Rogan, his vestments rustling softly like the whispering of holy voices, turned his head indicatively but unobtrusively and began to recite the *Sanctus*. Catching the priest's voice almost too late, he reached out his hand and rang the altar bell. The congregation knelt. The sound of their knees meeting the wooden kneeling boards echoed like a long-drawn-out roll of distant thunder. The golden flames which tipped the candles wavered and steadied. Then it was quiet. He was to pray for his father. Father Rogan had asked him to tell him about the accident, and that was easy, for he remembered it all; his father's brown suit, the packet of biscuits with the white paper wrapping and the red seal which he tried to stick on his coat for a badge, but it fell off. His father handed them to him outside the pub and he was drunk even then. There were two other men his father had met.

Is that the eldest? one asked.

The eldest and only, said his father.

He's very like you, Michael.

His father pretended to be affronted.

I hope not, he said truculently. They laughed. It was then his father handed him the biscuits.

He's a good lad, he said gravely as he did so.

It was a warm July day. The whitewashed wall of the public house gleamed hot and white in the sun, and while he waited he picked little flakes off it with his nail. When he grew tired he sat among the clover by the roadside and heard the insects humming. The fields were full of buttercups and daisies. Beyond them rose the hill with the mountain railway winding up towards the summit. It rose steeply with red sandstone cliffs and many furze bushes in sprawling yellow clumps. Here and there the sun flashed blindingly on the windows of small whitewashed cottages. His father came out at last and the two men were with him. They were singing. He frowned at them. They had been a very long time.

I supposed you'd given us up, his father said.

He looked down at the grass and sulked.

Well—then, his father said, casting round for something which would please him, we'll have a trip on the mountain railway—how's that?

He said all right without pretending to be much interested and the four of them set off. His father put his arm about his shoulders as they walked. He was disgruntled and hurt at being kept waiting and when his father lurched unsteadily it was an excuse.

You're drunk, he said.

I had a few, his father agreed tolerantly. It's our day out.

You mean it's your day out.

His father looked hurt.

Now, now, he said, squeezing his shoulder, you and I don't quarrel, son—do we. Life's too short.

He shouted at the other two in front.

Isn't that a fact . . . Joe . . . Dick?

What's that? they asked, turning around to grin. He began to sing life's too short to quarrel, hearts are too precious to break. He was in high good humour again and kept singing in snatches as they boarded the electric car. He stayed on the platform and the rest of the people laughed at him. But when the car started and the ticket collector ordered him aside, his humour became truculent and he began to argue. He heard his father using bad language and blushed scarlet with shame. Joe said to Dick: Prevail on him to come in before he gets us all arrested. His father came in with Dick. While they travelled he was very belligerent and kept abusing the conductor. The ticket collector went upstairs.

Didn't I pay my fare? his father demanded.

You did—of course, said Dick.

Like anybody else?

Like anybody else, Dick said. Now shut up like a good-mannered man.

I'll shut up when I bloody well like, his father said, tilting the bowler arrogantly over his eyes and rising.

Please yourself, Dick said with patience, but sit down anyway.

I'll sit or stand when I please, said his father, angrily, not at any man's behest. He pulled his arm free and went out on the platform. Joe looked imploringly at Dick.

For the love of God, he said, go out and fetch him in.

His father was on the platform, singing with drunken defiance. He saw him swaying and then Dick catching him by the arm. His father pulled away.

Go to hell, he said and leaned out. He heard the sharp concussive sound and his father was no longer on the platform. The brakes made a loud grinding noise which filled the whole car. When they stopped he jumped off and went racing back along the tracks. Dick overtook him. He pulled him back as he reached his father's body. There was the body but no head. The conductor said: The man was drunk; there's a warning about poles. He stuck out his head. He felt his face being pressed roughly against Dick's waistcoat button. At that moment, his eyes no longer on the body, he screamed. Someone said: Take the child away—you fool.

He heard Father Rogan's boots creak as he genuflected and rang the bell. The white Host was raised. He saw it poised for an instant against the bars of the tall white candles. Eight golden flames, the souls of the Elect stood still in worship. He tried to pray. But the paper fluttered against the weathered bars, lost its grip, and whirled in terror across the stones in the wind-raked field of the damned. He lowered his eyes. No matter how softly he flicked his wrist the bell wakened and hushed the church with echoes. It resounded in the body and chattered brightly in corners. He left it down with relief. Judge not and you shall not be judged, Father Rogan had said to him. It sounded frightening in the cold confessional. It came back now in the silence, after the din of the bell, a voice from a remote place speaking to him alone, so clearly that he looked around to see if it had been heard.

Did you love your father? Wasn't he kind to you?

He told people you won this in school and that for sports. Often he got angry but it was never for long. His mother said God help him, a kind word to him and you could twist him around your little finger. In the street you walked linking him and if you met the fellows you said this is my dad and you felt proud.

Yes, Father, he had said, his tears still falling. So inadequate was it, it felt almost like telling a lie.

If you loved him because he was good, how much more would God love him? We must not judge others, my son. God's mercy is infinite, and works in mysterious ways. Pray for your father and say to the Sacred Heart, when this terrible doubt troubles you, Sacred Heart of Jesus I place my trust in Thee. That will bring you comfort. You will do that, won't you?

Yes, Father.

For the moment he had felt at ease. But now it occurred to him that his mother loved him but that did not mean God would not send him to hell if he died in mortal sin. The doubts crept quietly upwards in him once more and he became so hot he felt weak and sick. The Host, the Living God, crackled very distinctly as Father Rogan's white fingers broke it. Behind him he could hear the quiet tread of feet as people came to the altar rails to receive. He tried hard to say Sacred Heart of Jesus but the blackened face appeared, smiled with gapped teeth, and dissolved before him. He pushed it violently from his mind. He rang the bell again when Father Rogan, striking his breast, his heavy eyes now almost closed, breathed the *Domine non sum dignus.* He thought he could pray and pray, all his life he might pray, but he would never know where his father was. Father Rogan did not know though he was pious and holy. God alone knew and God rarely told, except perhaps in visions of His saints, or in signs, or very occasionally in a secret half-heard whisper to the heart when you received Him in Holy Communion. One moment the sun beat down on the warm tracks, the people laughed, and you could tell people you were well or you were angry or you were hungry or you were sick. And then there was nothing at all; only a leg which could not walk and a mouth which was dumb and an eye which could not see. And somewhere inaccessible except to the dead themselves the flames leaped and the air was full of screams and God, no longer merciful or patient but terrible in majesty and Justice, called out a name which echoed from star to star.

Father Rogan turned around for the *Agnus Dei.* His stout white fingers held the communion particle over the ciborium. Father Rogan was looking at him curiously, waiting for him to go up to receive. But he could not rise. His eyes, resting on the tall candles behind the waiting figure of the priest, remained fixed there. Father Rogan delayed imperceptibly, then went down to administer to the people at the rails. He felt sick, but with an effort he rose and followed.

As he returned from the altar rails his eyes were drawn once more to the candle. The red point at the tip had now burned out. A thin column of smoke streamed up from it still. But the blackened wick had curled, acrid and damned, an unspoken message amid the golden beauty of the seven. He looked down at the priest's biretta. It lay before him on the altar steps. Soon he would have to take it up, kiss it, and hand it to the priest. But as he reached out his hand towards it he thought again of the candle and the biretta began to spin in front of him. It was a black and hideous face. The tassel parted in the middle and grinned widely at him. It began to roll down the white road. Steel tracks caught the sunlight and dazzled as they flung it back. Down the road rolled the head. Rolling and bouncing it rolled while he chased endlessly. It was exhilarating and he laughed. He caught up on it. Wielding his stick he began to roll it before him like a hoop. The wind, whistling past his ears, was odourous and hot like a furnace stream. Father Rogan, at the bottom of the steps now, crossed himself and began to recite the prayer for the dead. *De profundis clamavi, ad te Domine, Domine. . .*

No response came. Father Rogan looked around at the pale face, the tense figure. He was unaware of the priest's eyes. Before him loomed great gates, under which the head rolled. He shook them with his hands and screamed noiselessly. The road dipped steeply into the sulphur-smelling darkness, the smoke choked him. Vile hands reached out and laughter resounded. Down through the flames and past the exulting figures the head passed, bouncing, grinning, spitting, mocking God, gathering momentum. He watched, and all the time beat futilely at the gates. He let his stick fall beside him. Daddy, he repeated silently, lacerated now by his guilt, his unkindness. Daddy. They were the gates of Hell. Yet he wanted to follow.

Father Rogan saw the perspiration on his forehead. Later he would call him to his room.

Fiant aures tuae intendentes, said the priest, making the responses himself, *in vocem deprecationes meam.*

THE HALF-CROWN

THE man in the bookshop was suspicious. He had his hands in the pockets of his grey overall and he looked at you in a sharp knowing way which made you feel guilty.

"*A Hall and Knight's Algebra,*" Michael, embarrassed, said.

The eyes, cold and commercial, looked from the book to Michael. "Hocking it. Slipping it out of the house to flog it for cigarettes and the pictures," said the eyes. The hand took the book.

"A shilling," the man said, and sucked his tooth.

"That's not enough," Michael said, "it's worth more than that. It's worth three bob at least." The man turned the book over, pretending to examine it. He saw that Michael's sports jacket was too small for him and the ends of his flannel trousers were turned down in an attempt to conceal their shortness.

"Name and address?" he asked, as though absent-mindedly. That was written inside the cover. But if they really inquired and they got to know at home?

"What's that necessary for?" Michael countered. "You don't think I stole it?"

"I'm entitled to ask that," the man said. "Lots of books is pinched this time of the year. Besides," he added, "maybe your mammy doesn't know you're selling it." He used the word "mammy" very deliberately as an insult to Michael's self-esteem. "Well," he said, "how about one and sixpence?"

"It's worth more than one and six," Michael persisted doggedly. The man handed it back. "There you are," he said without interest, "take it or leave it." That was that.

The previous evening he had been so certain of getting at least half a crown that he had told Anne Fox he would meet her at the station. He had been out swimming with Mark, her brother, at Sandycove and when they came back she stood on the steps to talk to them. He had leaned over the borrowed bicycle with the togs and towel wrapped about the handlebars, enticed by her dark eyes, her slim bare knees, and moved by the cool and salty odour of his own body. He would risk a lot to be with her. Getting half a crown had seemed a small enough task. He thought she was very beautiful. At one point the thought so absorbed him that she said to him smiling, "A penny for them, Michael." But he had no words as yet for graciousness.

It had been the first thought to come into his mind when he was wakened too early that morning by his mother's hand stirring his shoulder. She was taking the child to the dispensary and wanted to be down early to be well placed in the queue.

"Michael son," she said at a quarter to eight. "Michael!" But the sun even at that hour was so strong in the bedroom he found it difficult to open his eyes. Without any intention of moving he said he was coming. At half past eight she again called him. "Your father has gone ages ago. You promised me you'd get up early," she said. But he pulled his shoulder away to show her how he hated her to touch him. Gradually over the past year he had felt hatred of her growing in him.

"I'm coming," he said angrily, "go and leave me alone." And when she had closed the door he turned over deliberately on his side. She had to be shown that shaking him would get her nowhere. But after a while, his anxiety to ask her for money had overcome his anger and he got up. She had fried bread for breakfast because it would save the butter, and when he sat down at table she served him with her hat and coat on. She had the baby in the pram. The rest of the children were with her married sister in the country. He said to her:

"We're going on an outing to-day. I want to know if you can give me half a crown."

"Half a crown," she said unhappily. "You got your pocket money on Saturday."

"You don't call one-and-sixpence pocket money."

That rebuffed her for a moment. She made another effort.

"Can't you borrow a bicycle somewhere?"

"We're going to Bray," he said. "The rest are going on the three o'clock train."

"Couldn't you arrange to meet them out there?"

Meet them out there? Tell them he had finished with school and could find no work and he couldn't help it if it meant being short of cash? He flung fried bread across the table.

"Keep your lousy half-crown," he had said, rising to go into the bathroom.

"Michael," she called after him, "you know if I had it I'd give it to you." He refused to answer. Then in a hurt tone she called to him, "I gave you two shillings last week." But he banged the door loudly. Later he had heard her take the pram down the steps by herself.

He stuffed the book back in his pocket. The sun, high over

the tall buildings and the summer crowds, beat down on his bare head. Even under the striped awnings outside the shops in Grafton Street it was intolerably hot. There was an aroma of coffee in the air to stir his appetite, and flowers blazed yellow and red in vendor's baskets. Near the Green two girls on bicycles looked at him with interest. One was a tidy piece but she wasn't as nice as Anne Fox. He wouldn't think of Anne Fox in that way. None of the girls was as nice as Anne Fox. She was different. She wouldn't do that—no—she wouldn't let you—no. But if he couldn't go to Bray maybe Dorgan would see her home. He got on easily with girls and when he knew Michael was soft on Anne he would make sure to cut in on him. Dorgan loved to do that. He would invent stories for the rest of the gang, which he could tell in a way that made it hard not to believe them. If he did he would break his bloody neck. Then of course the rest would think it was sour grapes, but it wasn't that at all. Anne wouldn't let you do that; she was a nice girl but she was soft on him too. He knew by the way she looked at him last night on the steps, and the way she leaned her head back a little so that he could see her soft warm shapely throat and the way she laughed at what he said to show she liked him to talk to her. So nice it had been last night on the high steps under the green-gold, cloud-crossed evening sky to ask her; and now it was all being bagged-up because of a lousy half-crown.

His father and mother were both at table. He walked through quietly to sneak the book back on the shelf. The baby was asleep in the pram. It had blobs of white ointment on its face. Bits of bun lay on its dress and coverlet. He took his place and his mother rose immediately to fetch his meal for him. The tassels of a faded green cover hung down beneath the tablecloth. There was a hole worn in the centre when the tablecloth was not on but you covered it with a fern pot and that was more or less all right. He looked at his father slyly with the idea of putting out a hint for some money but his father's face was not a good-humoured one—in fact—no—it wasn't. His father's face was moist and flabby. Though it was so warm he wore a dark suit and a butterfly collar which was respectable because of his calling. He was a clerk in the office of Joshua Bright & Son, Timber Merchants. In good humour he told stories which always ended in Mr. Bright saying, "Kavanagh, you're a man after my own heart. How on earth did you fix it? I'm certainly indebted," or words to that effect. It always made you want to kick both of them in the fanny. But Bright was not on the menu to-day. There was something else.

"If I've told you once," began his father, "I've told you a dozen times that a razor should be dried and cleaned when you've finished with it. No one with manners a cut above those of a pig would leave a razor in the condition mine was left in. I've never objected to you using it—though what in God's name you have to shave is beyond me—all I ask is that you dry it after you."

He remembered he had not dried it. He had left it down to put water in his hair in the absence of hair dressing and of course he forgot—well, he didn't exactly forget but he was in a bad humour over his mother.

"Razor?" he lied, pointlessly and brazenly. "I never touched your razor."

His father turned to his mother. "There's your rearing for you now," he said; "the lie springs easy to his lips. If he's going to sit there——"

His mother immediately tried to conciliate them. Too

quickly, in her desire to placate them his mother said, "You might have left it yourself, you were in such a hurry this morning."

"That's right," his father shouted, and let the knife and fork fall with a clatter on the plate, "stick up for him. Encourage him to deceive and defy his own father. I'll be a bloody lunatic before long between the pair of you."

"You can think what you like," Michael persisted. "It wasn't me."

"Michael," put in his mother.

"Then I suppose it was the cat," his father said with childish sarcasm, "or maybe it walked out of the case by itself. But I'll tell you one thing, you'll use it no more. You can get a razor of your own."

"I suppose you'll tell me how."

"Buy one. Do a little study to fit yourself for earning your keep."

"You must have studied a bit yourself in your day." Michael sneered. "You earn such a hell of a lot now."

He left the table. As he entered the next room a cup flew past his ear and shattered against the wall. It was unexpected and he jumped.

"You impertinent brat," his father yelled after him. He locked the door hastily.

He came out when he was certain his father had gone. His mother took his meal from the oven where she had put it to keep it hot. She had been crying. That sort of thing had never happened before.

"Have your meal, child," she said. "I don't know what's to become of us."

"I don't want it."

"It isn't right to answer your father like that; you should respect him. He works hard for what he gets."

"He knows how to hold on to it too."

She was silent. Then she said, "You know you'd get the half-crown if we had it. What were you ever denied that we had to give?"

"You can buy that baby in there sweet cake."

"A little penny bun. I'm ashamed of you, Michael."

That, unaccountably, slipped under his guard and stung him.

"You mind your own bloody business," he lashed back.

In St. Stephen's Green, children, their nurses watching them, were feeding the ducks from paper bags. And at the pond with the artificial sprays which spurted threads of pearly bright water into the thirsty air, children were sailing a boat. Michael lounged with his hands in his pockets. They were catching the train now.

"Michael Kavanagh is awful to be late like this," the girls were saying with angry little jerks of their heads, and the fellows were saying, "Oh, he'll come, don't bother, let's get a carriage." They were going to Bray to swim and after to lie in the bracken. They were going to eat ice cream and drink lemonade which the boys would buy for the girls, and eat sandwiches and make tea which the girls would bring for the boys. Anne would lie in the bracken. For the length of his own afternoon he could watch the people sleeping with newspapers over their faces and look at the flowers which blazed with a barren and uncommunicative joyousness. The sculptured face of Mangan brought some lines to his mind. "I could scale the blue air. I could walk . . . climb . . . I could . . ." How the hell did it go? That was school. You knew these things when you sat for Leaving Cert. and then after a while you wondered how the hell did it go. You left school and watched the advertisements.

"Junior clerk reqd. rep. firm Hons. Leaving Cert. Knowledge book-keeping asset. 15/- weekly to start. Good prospects."

Queue with the rest; don't stammer—oh—don't stutter— think, oh, think. Cool—be cool and smile respectfully. Self-possession is nine-tenths of the law.

Your mother had pressed your suit and sat up into the small hours ironing and darning. She had already begun a Novena to Saint Anthony. (O please, Saint Anthony, send him work: O please. O sweet and good Saint Anthony intercede for my boy.) Your father gave you advice. He told you, take off your hat and smile easily and pleasantly. Don't fidget or sit on the edge of the chair, which wasn't to say, of course, that you were to put your feet on the desk. He had had a word with Gussy Gallagher who was said to have tons of influence since he hit it lucky in the auctioneering business. He was reputed to be a brigadier-general or something in the Knights of Columbanus. Now and then your mother looked across.

"Pay attention to what your father is telling you," she would say. When she ironed late at night like that her hair fell in straggles over her face, her breath caught her now and then, her forehead so white showed moistly in the steamy light.

As you sat waiting to be interviewed you kept saying like an idiot over and over again something silly—like:

"When Richelieu attained to office he was faced with the task of building a French navy."

Like when you were a child you went to the shop repeating in case you might forget: A pint of milk—a tin of beans—a duck loaf—and a half-pound of margarine and say the margarine is for baking. (That was a lie, but it was only a little white lie if your mother told you to tell it.)

But in the end someone else, like Harte or Joe Andrews, always got the job. Joe Andrews didn't know much about Richelieu, but he knew someone on the selection board with a bit more pull than Gussy Gallagher or Saint Anthony.

Knowledge weakened with winter, sickened with spring, withered and died in the hot July sun, giving place to new growths, to the contemplation of women, to long vacant hours, to quick greeds and slow lusts and jealous incessant neediness.

He sat down on one of the benches which were placed at secluded intervals along the quiet path. His mother was a silly bitch and his father a skinflint. His mother went out with his father to the pictures once a week and this was the night. It was the only night they went out but they could stay at home to-night because the other children were away and he was damned if he was going to stay in to mind the baby. That would be one way of getting his own back. The whole set-up was a bloody cod.

There was a thin white line running down the right side of his face, from his nose to the corner of his lips. He tried to relieve the tautness from time to time by rubbing his face with his hands, but failed because it welled up from inside him. Over him hung a wealth of almond blossom and opposite to him was a laburnum tree. It showered with perfect grace of movement to the tips of its trailing branches. Near it sat an old man and a child. He was a white-haired, serene-faced old man, whose ample waistcoat was crossed by two golden chains. On one end of the chain hung a watch. The little child was playing with it. She put it to her ear, listened, laughed. "Tick tock, tick tock," the old man said, making an attempt to imitate the sound. Frequently he bent down to chuck her under the chin or smile at her. Growing tired of the watch, she put her hand in his pocket to pull out a pair of glasses, a white handkerchief and a silver coin. The glasses and handkerchief were discarded, but she kept the coin. When she threw it, it flashed in the sun; when it fell, it rang musically on the path and rolled round and round. It staggered in circles before flopping down. The old man, whom you knew to be old more by the stringy looseness of the neck behind his white butterfly collar than by any sign of age in the bright face, smiled an invitation to Michael to enjoy the antics of the child. But Michael only hated the child. He hated the child because a foolish and indulgent old man allowed it to play carelessly with a precious piece of silver. The milled edges of a half-crown were strong and comforting. You could stand a girl's fare and buy her ice cream, or buy cigarettes to smoke after a swim, and fish and chips to eat from a paper bag on the way home with the lads at night. The coin went up and down and he followed it greedily with his eyes. Sometimes it fell, a bright though tiny star, out of the child's reach, and the child would toddle across innocently to retrieve it. Sometimes when it fell, it staggered clumsily towards Michael. When the game had gone on for some time the old man lost interest and began to nod. Michael looked up and down the path. A keeper was examining a flower bed some distance away. There was nobody near. But to rise, take up the coin and walk away quickly— that would be too obvious. The child might cry, or the old man open his eyes at the wrong moment. With half-closed eyes he followed the course of the coin.

To steal a half-crown could be mortal or venial. Three conditions were required for mortal sin and these were: (1) grave matter: (2) perfect knowledge; (3) full consent. It would be mortal to steal it from a poor man, but venial to steal it from a rich man, because it was dependent on the gravity of the injustice done. Not that he cared whether it was mortal or venial because he had committed sins of impurity which were always mortal and killed the soul, and it was eight months since his last confession. Automatically he almost said, "and I accuse myself of my sins." When the slide went click in the darkness the priest didn't say a penny for them he said well my child and with tongue stuck to roof and sweat of shame you had to tell. If you were caught you were a (not-nice-word) thief.

The coin fell and rolled towards him. He watched it. It curved, glittering, towards his left. Gingerly he reached out his foot and stopped it. Then he looked sharply at the old man, whose eyes were still closed. He bent and picked it up.

"Go on," he whispered to the child when she came near him, "hump off." The face upturned to him was tiny and questioning. He could have raised his boot and crushed it without caring. But her bewilderment frightened him. When she began to cry he jumped up and said to her: "Here—we'll look for it in the grass."

He was earnestly searching along the verge when the old man stood beside him.

"Poor little pet," he said, "what's the matter now?"

"She lost her half-crown. I think it rolled in here."

They hunted for a considerable time. Michael kept his face averted. His heart thumped. He was afraid the old man might see it there thumping against his ribs, pulsing in his neck, calling out thief, thief, so loudly that it must surely be heard. But the child began to sob and the old man comforted her by promising to bring her off to buy ice cream. After some time he told Michael he would have to leave it for the sweeper. "Finders keepers," he said regretfully but pleasantly as he was going.

Waiting impatiently while the old man and the child went off, Michael sat down again. He had no notion of the time. He should have asked the old fool before he went. They had gone in the direction of the station, but he would not dare to go that way lest they should meet again. The old man would want to chat. Where did he live? Was he still at school? What were his intentions? Suitable openings were hard to find for a young man standing on the threshold of life. A grunt, A stammer. There were no other answers to these things, none that he had found. They were simple expressions of amiability which always made the machinery of his mind lumber and clank, defeated and chaotic. He could never find responses. He was afraid if the old man spoke to him, he would blurt out, "I took the half-crown and I'm sticking to it. You can do what you like about it." So he sat for half an hour and then went off in the opposite direction, taking a roundabout way to the station. He passed the university where Mark would soon begin to study to be a doctor. He always had money. Mark would never need to put his foot on a half-crown dropped by a child in a public park.

The street was so quiet he could hear his own footsteps echoing, and the building itself seemed peacefully asleep. There was a smell of dust and a sunlit silence. He thought of cool waters, of Anne Fox in her red bathing costume raising her round arms to let cool water fall from them glitteringly. She would climb Bray Head in her light cotton frock, slim knees bending, a sea-fragrance about her. It would not be easy to find them. She might go anywhere about the Head to lie in the bracken. She might lie in the bracken with Dorgan. He would have to search and search.

He hastened up the steps to the station, as though by hastening he could persuade the train to leave any earlier, or be with her any sooner. But when he reached the top he stood still. Just turning away from the booking office, holding the child by the hand, was the old man. The child wanted to carry the tickets. On the steps, an impassable barrier, stood guilt and terror. Instinctively and immediately he moved away.

At the corner of the Green, leaning against one of the pillars which had held the ornamental chains that one time bordered the pavement, he remained for a long time. He knew it was after six o'clock because people were passing in clusters on bicycles, and the hunger pains in his belly were worse. He should have taken his dinner. He was staring at the sky, golden and tranquil behind barred clouds, when his mother stopped beside him. She had been shopping and was pushing the pram with the baby in it. He knew it was she but barely moved to acknowledge her. Let her see him miserable. Let her see that he had only a corner to stand at and a sky to stare into. It would hurt her and that was something to know. Once he had loved them. When he was young, before the other children came along, he and his mother had often waited for his father at that very corner with a flask of tea and sandwiches and hot currant buns. They used to go into the Green to sit on the grass and have a picnic. But now he hated them. He had nothing to say to them. He had hated them for a long time now but they refused to recognise it. His mother waited. Then she said, "A penny for them, Michael."

Anne Fox had said that too, and now she was lying in the

bracken with Dorgan. He made a sullen mask of his face and refused to answer. After a while, this time more urgently, she said, "Michael."

He grunted and shrugged.

"The baby isn't well," she began, once again placating him, trying to soften him, to bring him back to her. "I think I'll stay in to-night. You can go to the pictures instead. Make it up with your father at tea and then the pair of you can go off together."

"What is there to make up?" he asked. "You make me sick."

Hesitantly she suggested: "You weren't very nice to him at dinner."

"He wasn't very nice to me—was he?"

He looked around as he asked and was shocked to see tears in her eyes. But she averted her head and began to walk. He lagged behind, refusing to walk beside her. He saw in hunger and misery the squat steeple of the Methodist church, and over it the sky crossed regularly with clouds—a painted sea. Girls in the sea were slim and lovely. Girls in the sea had straight slim shapely legs. He looked at his mother's legs. They were very thin. They were encased in cheap unfashionable stockings, woolly, yellow in colour, wrinkled above the calves, much darned and dragged at the ankles. Her skirt was uneven as it swung about them. He watched the effort of her short step-by-step movement. He could not remember ever having looked at his mother's legs before. Now it stabbed him like a sword. His throat contracted. He searched for something brutal to say, something to protect himself against this fresh and unexpected onslaught of pain. She walked with her thin back towards him, her hands guiding the pram.

"We'll have to hurry home," she said brightly; "your poor father will be ages waiting."

He hoped to God she had wiped her eyes. He did not want people to see her. She quickened her pace and panted with the initial push.

"I have an egg for your tea," she added.

The brutality in him subsided. An egg for his tea. It made him want to laugh. But it also made him want to stretch out his hand to her, to touch her, to tell her he was sorry. But there were no words. He cast around for words. But when he even tried to think of them the grinding and turmoil in his head only became worse. Then his fingers touched the stolen half-crown. A flush of shame and unworthiness crept sullenly into his cheeks. It was suddenly without value. It could not buy what he wanted. Because he hardly knew what he wanted. He struggled with his own tears. He watched her now with immense tenderness, sorry for her, aching with love for her. But still something, his pride or his great shyness, would not permit him to speak to her or even to walk beside her.

In that way they went home; she walking ahead and unwitting, and he, who had no words for anything except churlishness or anger, followed silently.

MERCY

IN HIS own good time, in His own unpredictable way.
Martin Quinn. His soul and the souls of all the faithful de-
parted, through the Mercy of God . . . Martin you are gone
oul'butty and I'm not long for the road. All our sins for long
enough was sinned together.

Morning sun shining brightly and warmly outside; tall
houses leaning over the street; bricks with age, dark and
burned looking, but here and there coloured strangely from
weather, pale red and orange and slaty blue. After dimness of
church traffic loud and repelling, light too strong, sun-warmth
seeping through clothes. Wait now.

He touched the money in his pocket, hesitated, then with
decision turned towards the vestry. The clerk, who was putting
away vestments, closed the press and came over. He explained
to the clerk.

"I want to have a Mass said—for Martin Quinn." Feeling
there was something missing, he fumbled a moment before he
thought of the phrase he wanted. "Recently deceased," he
added, satisfied.

"Certainly," the clerk said and reached for a book.

"And I want a second one offered."

"Two Masses for the repose of the soul of Martin Quinn."

"No. The second is for someone else. I . . ."

"Yes?"

"I don't know his name."

"That happens to us all when we get on," the clerk said gently. "We forget in spite of ourselves. You can have the second mass offered for your special intention."

"Would that be for his soul?"

"That would be your special intention. A Mass to be offered for the soul of your—friend. It's the same thing."

While the clerk wrote in the book, he took a ten shilling note from his pocket and left it on the desk. His offering. That would leave him short. But God, who fed the sparrows, would not see him hungry.

"Thank you," said the clerk. "They will be the 8 o'clock Mass to-morrow and the 10 o'clock on Wednesday."

He put the beads in his pocket, dipped his hand in the holy water font and walked slowly down the steps. It had been a great shock, the priest turning from the altar and saying: "Your charitable prayers are requested for the repose of the soul of Martin Quinn, for whom this Mass is offered." After getting through the winter too. And he wouldn't have known a word because he wouldn't have gone to the Mass only the letter from the Ministry of Pensions had arrived that morning and he wanted to bring it to Fenlon. He had attained the age of seventy it said. He had, begod—no thanks to them. For long he had looked forward to it, talking about it to Fenlon and the rest, thinking how he wouldn't let on about the watching job he did now and then, in case it would interfere with it, wishing and worrying his few years away. And then this last few days

he did not want to get it at all. And last night in the light of
his torch a large brown rat had sat and grinned at him. On
the ledge of the clock where he punched his card it sat, eye-
ing him, cerebrating. It was a summons. Like a crow on a telegraph wire or a beetle tapping its message through a wall.

He took the bottle from his pocket and went around the side
of the church to fill it from the barrel with the rough white
cross chalked upon it. He wanted holy water for his room. For
that matter he could take some with him to the cutting to-
night. It was lonely to sit in the watch box remembering bits
and scraps of things, recalling faces, an old man not knowing
the day nor the hour. A week of nights he had guarded the
piled-up rubble, the tarred wooden sets, seeing the red lamps
of warning growing pale with each dawn and waiting for the
first footsteps to ring with morning hollowness on the pavement. Lately he would fancy them as the receding footsteps of
life, or the approaching feet of death. With each dawn judgment came nearer. In the surface of the water were reflected
the uncombed grey locks, the filmed, sleep-denied eyes, the
grey stubble on his cheeks. Then disintegrated in broken rip-
ples as he plunged the bottle below the surface. He pushed the
cork in tightly and went down High Street. The cutting was
deep. It exposed the tunnels which honeycombed that part
of the city, vaults which radiated from the Cathedral, ancient
sewers which ran down Winetavern Street to the river. Once
they had been drinking cellars and rebel plotting dens. Now
the rats had taken possession. He remembered the clock. It
hung beside a partition which sealed off an exposed vault.
It was part of his duty to go down to punch it every hour. That
was to make sure he inspected it. A pneumatic drill spattered
as he passed, and the man nodded to him. "Bad luck to you,"
he murmured. But he was referring to the rats.

They were seated on the carved seats. Fenlon, Reeves and Hanlon, secluded in the sunny courtyard from the constantly passing people and traffic. Hanlon had turned a little away from the other two and leaned on a stick. Cronies. He was in no humour to join them, but he had the letter.

"More power, Fred," Fenlon greeted. "Sit down and take the weight off your legs." The sun-warmed stone felt comfortable against his back. He put the spectacles on the end of his nose, unfolded the letter, read Frederick Toner, Top Back, 23 Fenian Lane off High Street, Dublin, and passed it without enthusiasm to Fenlon.

"From the Government," he explained. "I got it at last."

"An unlucky breed," Reeves stuck in.

"But I can't get the gist of it at all; and there's a week's hard work filling in answers to questions."

"Them fellows go on with a lot of nonsense," Reeves complained, "and if you venture to ask them a question you get nothing but the height of abuse. Johnny-jump-ups with a plaster of fountain pens and the dung still fresh on their hobnailed boots."

"I'll fill in what you want," Fenlon said, "and bring it back to you to-morrow."

Age had failed to undermine Fenlon's great air of confidence, and the alertness which the waxed military moustache gave to his face was not entirely false. He knew his onions. No flies nor fears on Fenlon. But tell them.

"Poor Martin Quinn is dead."

"For God's sake. Where did you hear that?"

"At ten o'clock mass. It was read from the altar."

There was a pause during which they raised unanimous hats.

"I didn't hear he was complaining," Reeves said, troubled.

"Nor I."

"That was a great butty of yours, Fred."

"He was. We soldiered together. The Boer War and after that in France. He was the heart of the rowl."

"He never looked after himself," Reeves said. "If he had he'd have been good for many a year yet." Aye. And if wishes were horses, beggars would ride. He could never warm to Reeves. An unsuccessful cattle jobber, generous to a fault in his day if you were fool enough to believe all the oul' guff he talked about himself. For myself, I never saw much of it. And a great man with the women—aye.

"Mind you," said Fenlon, "he had a power of money at one time."

"He had—enough money to build a chapel."

"More money than sense."

"God's truth, some people have all the luck." Reeves burst out, "the world is badly divided."

Divil thank the begrudgers. There was no mean drop in you, Martin. Spend it like water when you broke out. That time when the eldest daughter got married. The pair of us on the batter for a fortnight. At it all night and then up to the market first thing in the morning. And your wife scouring the town for us. Poor woman, it was her money we were spending. Sheila Cassidy the publican's daughter from Macken Street. It put her early in her grave, Martin, the carry-on of the pair of us. Lovely she was at that time with her golden head of hair. Wistfully he murmured.

"She'd charm the birds down out of the trees," not meaning to say it aloud. That was age, too. They looked at him curiously.

"I mean his wife that's gone," he added in explanation.

"Sheila Cassidy," Reeves said. "That's where the money

came from. You'll find he still had a bit in the stocking. He always got the height of attention from the family."

"There'll be a contest between the daughters over his few ha'pence now," Fenlon said, "if I'm any judge in the matter."

Holy Hughie Hanlon in his greasy dustcoat turned a grey-bearded face with its gentle contemplative eyes and addressed them for the first time. As he moved, the rosary beads in his pocket, which he was forever silently and secretly telling, rattled betrayingly.

"You will never see so many prayers as at a poor man's wake," he said, "but where there is a little money there is nothing but fighting and cursing."

"Well then," Toner remarked with forced gaiety, "I'll get the prayers anyway."

"Me too—for what they're worth," said Fenlon. "I came into this world without a stitch and I'll go out of it without one."

That was true. You left it all behind. Naked and alone you walked the road to hereafter. Holy Hughie Hanlon smiled contentedly.

"There will none of us be heavy burdened on the road to heaven," he said.

At least there was conversation here. Not like at the cutting in the silence of the night, or lying down to sleep in his room with only the old mongrel scratching and showing its age too. Here the cathedral rose behind him, full of beauty and strength, and the trees were freshly in leaf. The apple blossom too was fresh and good to look on. Winter the worst enemy had passed. There were flowers once more and sunlight and children to run past now and then with shrieks of young laughter. Fear would have seemed far off, were it not for the patter of pneumatic drills which came to them, persistent but subdued;

jabbing with tenacious teeth which ripped raw wounds in the now untrafficked street. They would not let him forget. He thought of the rat. Then he thought of Martin, burdened with their common sin, and God knows what light or heavy load besides (had he the priest?) walking alone now the road to his judgment. He watched Hanlon's face for some time, and saw the lips moving soundlessly. They said he was a bit soft in the head. There must be great peace of mind in it anyway to let a man pray tranquilly like that. And no loneliness. He was about to tell them about the rat.

He said, thinking again of the scraping he heard every time he went down into the cutting and the flopping sound they made when they jumped.

"I got a bad shaking up last night."

"What was that?" Reeves asked.

But a young man, wearing his flesh proudly, not fearing rats, came towards them.

"Your son," Reeves said.

It was difficult for a moment to tear his thoughts from the thing in his mind, to look up at the young man who paused to greet them.

"I thought you were watching this week," his son said, "I didn't expect to find you here."

"I am watching, but I went to Mass instead of going to bed."

"A holy and wholesome thought," his son said brightly. His son's brightness embittered him, so that it crept into his voice.

"It was. A good friend of mine is gone."

"Who's that?"

"Martin Quinn."

"Is that a fact?"

"Well," his son added, "there's little the matter with you

anyway. You're looking younger every day—what do you say, Mr. Fenlon?"

Encourage him. If he stops the watching he'll be a burden —what I never was.

"We'll have to shoot him," Fenlon said agreeably, "that's the only solution."

My son. My tall broad rearing a labourer in the Corporation, in a fair way of becoming a ganger too, so they say. Faith and I watched you for more than long enough, me fine bucko Barney from Ballydehob. When it was daddy-I-this and daddy-me-that. A cute brew ever he was. Snooping round now about the pension, trying to find out if I'm picking up the few shillings that I never let on about. But it's too much trouble to you to call up to the room to me, to sit an hour with your father that reared you. Still my son for all that; my hope, my disillusionment.

"Your sister was with me last week," he said, giving him the rub. "She brought me a drop of brandy to keep in the house against sickness." Then more warmly, hoping for sympathy, falling into the trap experience could never teach him to avoid, he added "I've been taking little turns." His heart. But it found no chink in the bright metallic armour of boisterous encouragement.

"Begod then," his son said, "I hope you told her you'd drink it while you had your health and your strength." He let a great guffaw out of him. "I'll be getting along," he said. "I'll drop up to you one of these days."

"You will, when it's too late."

"That's a fine boy," they said smiling after him.

Aye. Fine for himself. Look after No. 1. Still—my son. Something of me there; me prudent; me looking after the pence. A ganger he would be. Then he would know the distrust of the men and feel the cold shoulder. He could have sat a few minutes for decency's sake if not for mine. Wouldn't the ganger's job wait a few minutes. I sat long enough with you child. Couldn't he have asked me to walk down the road a stretch with him, to talk things over, to tell him what had happened. But it would be no use telling him about the rat. He would only laugh it away. Youse don't need me now, none of you. I'm not wanted now. When the mother goes, all goes.

"If he's half the man his father was, he'll do," he said. Sadly, bitterly, wearily, he said it.

After a while Reeves remembered. "You had something to tell us," he said. But the mood was gone. They would not understand. They would not be interested to grasp the deeper meaning of what he had to say; to know he had received a summons.

"Nothing," he evaded. "A bit of a dream. I disremember."

"I had a peculiar dream myself last night," holy Hughie Hanlon said. "I was dead, if you please, and was on my way to heaven."

"Do you think you'll go to heaven when you die, Hughie?"

"I have that hope," Hughie said simply.

His calm belief nettled Fenlon, so that he said with sudden bitterness:

"I hope you're all not disappointed. I mean about your novenas and your retreats, your heavens and your hells."

Reeves had been smiling but now he stopped.

"A nice collection," Fenlon pursued, "the three of you. Afraid of God and afraid of the devil. If there was a God up above there he'd burn the whole bloody lot of you—out of malice begod."

"Do you believe in nothing at all?" Reeves asked him.

"I do," Fenlon said. "I believe I'm like the tree—where I fall I rot."

There was an embarrassed silence. A young man might be careless of God's judgment and condemnation, but an old man nearing his end should be cautious of pride. Toner's hand touched the holy water bottle in his pocket. Shame uprose and with it fear.

"There's no call for that sort of talk," he said uneasily.

"I was asked a question," Fenlon returned blandly.

By way of apology Reeves said, "Pay no attention to him, Fred. He's trying to rise you. He doesn't mean a bit of it."

Toner made an angry movement. Reeves expected he would ask them to have a pint with him on account of his having got his wages for the week's watching that morning. Reeves could wait then. He had come to them with the weight of his three score and ten, seeking reassurance and companionship, but what was there in them in the heel of the hunt. Fenlon's mockery, Hanlon's half cracked holiness, Reeves' glib tongue smoothing things over because he did not want him to be angered. There was no warmth now in the sun. The seat was hard and painful against his back. He could not sit longer with them. It was bad to be lonely when you were alone. It was more unbearable to be lonely in company. He rose brusquely and broke the unhappy silence by saying "I may as well go home and wet myself a cup of tea."

A little boy bumped into him, stopped to disentangle himself, and ran off again crying, "All in—all in, the game is broke up," a ragged little wretch with most of his three score and ten outspread enviably before him, his innocence as yet unsullied. No need there for the rosary beads and the offering of Masses. Fenlon's way was an easy one if it were only true—a sleep with no waking. At the end of the road came the shroud and the cold clay. Eyes rolled from their sockets and flesh peeled and putrefied. No gracefulness there, no clean crumbling like the tree. Pollution and the dark mouths of maggots, the stealthy scraping of rats. Body not like strong straight unsuffering tree, no. Because I was paid to-day youse are looking after me, thinking I might have asked youse to have a pint atself, not knowing that me money is given for Masses that I, God help me, and Martin too has more need of than youse have of drink. And that's the deep interest youse have in me.

O Christ your face is bent on me, and your forehead thunderous beneath Its thorns. Mother of God me strength is all gone out of me, me body is feeble, me flesh is filthy, me soul is scarred and stained with a rime of sins. Holy Mother pray for me a sinner now and at the hour of my death. Jesus, Mary and Joseph assist me, now and in my last agony. Jesus, Mary and Joseph may I breathe forth my soul in peace with you. In peace. The book of my deeds is read and then there is heaven or there is hell. Not like the tree the soul which burns forever, not like the tree the sin rotted soul. As he passed under the apple blossom he heard Reeves complaining bitterly.

"There he goes now, with his week's money weighing down his pocket, and never asked us if we'd a mouth on us."

The night was mild. In front of his watchbox the brazier glowed warmly. No one came near him except a passerby who delayed a moment to light a cigarette, offered him one, and remarked casually the old mongrel which lay curled beside him. He had taken it with him for company. It was old and useless but it came where he bid it. He rooted in his pocket and showed the blackened clay pipe in explanation. "Never could touch them sir," he said, leaning forward painfully a moment from the dark warmth of the box. "Thank you all the same."

The other moved away. A well-set-up young blade in evening dress with a cargo of drink aboard. A student, he thought, on his way to some diversion. They were the divils too. Drowsily he gazed after the figure until it receded first from his vision and then slowly altogether from his mind. He gazed until the seat he was sitting on was no longer warm and comfortable but suddenly cold and hard.

The sun was shining without heat in a clear sky, the little children ran past him, the apple blossom showered before him in delicate beauty. Martin Quinn was sitting beside him. Seeing Martin beside him made his heart pump erratically.

"Martin," he began, trying to bring himself to speak it. But the sentence finished itself in his mind only, "you're dead."

Martin's face was tired and white. He wore the uniform of the Irish Guards.

"What are you doing here, Martin?"

"I can't get to heaven with the weight of my sins," Martin said.

"Isn't there Mercy?"

Martin smiled. "Do you remember the retreat from Mons when we shot down the Scottish Borderers. Because of what we heard they done on Bloody at Bachelor's Walk."

"Because they opened fire and murdered our flesh and blood. I do."

"Do you remember you and I came on one of them in a wood?"

"I've remembered little else all day. He taped what we were up to. He tried to hide."

"What did he say when we cornered him?"

"He said, we're on the same side in this, Paddy. He said, Mercy Paddy, for sweet Jesus' sake Mercy."

"And what did we do, Fred?"

"We shot him in the head," Toner answered, his voice dying to nothing.

"You see," Martin Quinn said, "Mercy." He gripped his sleeve. His half-eaten fingers which the gnawing rats had befouled, were cold.

"That was murder, Fred. We rifled the Temple of the Holy Ghost. Watch now and see it fall."

"What are you blathering about?" Toner asked in terror.

"Watch now."

Over the mountains, a small black cloud formed. It began to grow. As it grew and moved forward towards them it blotted out the sun, smearing the sky with alternate streaks of soot and blood. The traffic had stopped and the people, tumbling from cars and buses, were running away. But they made no sound. Silence lay on the street. His son rushed by without turning his head and in front of him Reeves gesticulated and pointed to the sky, while Fenlon shook his head in angry denial. Holy Hughie Hanlon knelt on the cobbles, his beads about his wrists, his face smiling and upturned. Then the railings bordering the close buckled as though with heat and pitched forward.

"Martin," he tried to say, "Martin—tell them I had a Mass said for his soul, tell them, Martin." But his lips moved futilely and made no sound at all.

"The temple of the Holy Ghost," Martin pointing upwards at the cathedral said, "Look what we done."

He looked up. The spire tottered crazily. All the rest had gone. He looked at Martin's face. A wide grin distorted it and the left eye socket was bloody and empty where the rats had ravaged it. As the stonework split and toppled he held his hands above his head. "Jesus protect me," he cried. In the darkness his body sweated its fear, his heart pounded and sickened him. The smell of sulphur grew bodingly. He said struggling, it's a dream, I know it's a dream. Christ deliver me from the terror of this thing.

He beat about him with his arms, fighting with all his strength towards wakefulness. His opening eyes, anticipating the still, warm silence of his bedroom, sought hungrily for comfort and anchorage the statue of the Sacred Heart, one hand upraised, the other pointing mutely to the sword-pierced Heart. But there was no statue, no spot of light which the small red oil lamp always projected on to the crumbling ceiling. Only darkness and the hard seat. Wait—

The dog whined and brushed against his leg. His fingers sought its rough, hairy coat. But it was to comfort himself, not the dog. Then he was aware once more of the red glow of the coke fire, the yellow smoke drifting thinly towards him, and beyond it the red lamps of warning strung out on either side of the cutting. A dream. There was a wealth of meaning behind that if you only delve deep enough. All things, auguries, omens, signs; a crow on a telegraph wire, a snapped picture cord, a brown rat on a clock. "Good boy," he said to the dog. "Good chap." Its upturned, rheumy eyes fixed him with unremitting loyalty. Painfully, because of his heart, he said to it, stroking it roughly.

"Whistle and I'll come—yes—whistle and I'll come." It was by way of a vague joke. It was his long habit, in pain and danger, to make a joke. His watch told him it was past the hour. But he hesitated. Let them wait for him now, the cute brew who employed him, their clock which spied on him, the rats who coveted him.

"Where's the bottle," he asked the dog, "where did we leave it?" He rummaged in the box, took out a bottle and peered at it. There was a white liquid in it. The milk for when he was wetting his cup of tea. He sighed.

"I've no memory," he complained, "no memory these times at all." He rooted again and found the bottle of holy water under the sack covering in the corner of the seat. He sprinkled it about him. A drop sizzled on the fire.

"In the name of the Father and of the Son," he breathed, "and of the Holy Ghost." Then he grunted and rose.

"We'll pay our respects to the clock," he said. The dog ambled after him.

It was dark outside the radius of the coke brazier. The bells of the Cathedral chimed to mark the half hour, echoed in the empty street, and dispersed into nothingness under the thin stars. He picked his way among scattered, tarry sets, over mounded earth and crusted pipes which exhaled an odour of stale gas, stumbling sometimes and stopping when his heart made the effort too difficult. Under his feet passages honeycombed the earth. They radiated from the Cathedral with their coffined bodies in family vaults, historic fragments scattered about the stone web, decayed wings left and forgotten by the spider. At the entrance to the tunnel the dog stopped and growled. The electric torch played from wall to wall. They were dry. A scraping sound. The rat. "Come on," he commanded, "in we go."

His torch cleaved a path of brightness before him and made the darkness outside its beam more sinister and oppressive. With the earthly smell in his nostrils, he thought of a new dug grave.

I had a Mass said for you, Martin, and one for him, whoever he was. And when I'm finished the watching I'll go to the altar for him. I'll tell the priest in confession that I shattered the temple of the Holy Ghost. You see after all the years I know how to confess it now. And he'll say what do you mean my child, calling me his child and I old enough to be his grand-

father, and I'll say I shot a man in cold blood, father, and for these and all my grievous sins I am sorry. As they walked the dog sniffed and whined. The dog did not want to go on. He played his torch on the partition and found it still intact and untouched. His heart pumped fiercely as he did go. Who would go near it in the darkness? "All's well," he said to the dog, "we can go." But as he put his card in the clock the sudden scurry of tiny claws caused him to jerk violently. Pain shot across his chest, pain overpowering and blinding, so that he sank first on one knee, and then pitched forward. The torch shattered, he lay in the darkness, gasping for breath and fighting desperately the seizure, praying it would pass. The barking of the dog reverberated from wall to wall, filling the tunnel with noise. The sharp stabs of sound beat in his head. He lay in the noise-filled darkness, sweating his pain, praying assist me now and in my last agony. Not like the tree the body felled and suffering, the soul straining to its judgment. Claws they had to dig the holy ground, eyes to pry out flesh and entrails, teeth to ravage the toppled temple of the Holy Ghost. Is it me own blood I'm lying in or the holy water bottle I broke when I fell? Jesus Mercy, is it me poor heart has burst like a blood-filled balloon inside of me? Mass I had said for Martin Quinn and for him. And for mercy him. Mary help.

In His own good time. In His own unpredictable way.

The dog stood trembling beside him, whining its fear, watching helplessly while he died. At the scrape of tiny feet or any stealthy movement it barked furiously. Throughout the hours it stood by his side. It stood whining, terror-stricken, guarding him, keeping them at bay, until morning came and with it the echoing of the first, lonely-sounding footsteps on the pavement above.

DUBLIN FUSILIER

MARTY came swinging across town. Beneath the tall lamps and the broad white-faced clocks, by picture houses and odourous restaurant gratings, under the pillar where what was left of Nelson posed proudly against the sky, came what was left of Marty. The General Post Office pushed out its ponderous chest, and Marty did likewise. In the darkness white faces passed him, warm scents assailed him, shoulders brushed his shoulder. A newsboy bawled in his ear "*Herald* or *Mail*, sir." But Marty walked his own path in his own city, the present like a soft mist trailing past him. For Marty and Nelson were aloof. Nelson on his pillar stuck his head a little higher up into the dark arch of the night, and his stony fingers were curled irrevocably on his sword. And beneath him marched Marty with his satchel of grenades. Both bore arms always.

Marty with his pale foxy face, the nose of a snipe, the chest of a pigeon, the gait of a halty mongrel, walked his own lonely inaccessible way. There was a drop on the end of his nose, which he removed from time to time by wiping with the back of his hand.

Tramp, tramp, tramp, came Marty the Dublin Fusilier. Pride in me heart, said Marty, and porter in me belly. Tramp, tramp, tramp, thunderously across the city came Marty.

"Tell me, me dear Lord Roberts," says Queen Victoria, "whose them?"

"Them, ma'am," says Lord Roberts, "is the Black Watch."

"Hmm," says the Queen.

Tramp, tramp, tramp.

"And who," says the Queen, "is them?"

"Them, ma'am," says Lord Roberts, "is the Coldstream Guards."

"Hmm," says the Queen.

Tramp, tramp, tramp.

"Quick," says the Queen, plucking at his arm, "whose them?"

"Them, ma'am," says Lord Roberts, "is the Dublin Fusiliers."

"Jasus," says the Queen, "them's Troops!"

Marty began to sing *Tipperary.*

"It's a long way, to Tipperary, it's a long way to go."

"Are you going far?" asked the voice. It was dark on the bridge and hard to see. Marty squinted from his height of five foot seven at a silver button and a big helmet. He halted. "Atten-shun," he bawled. So the policeman grinned broadly at the thin, sick face under the peaky cap, and the sharp nose with its pendulent drop.

"So that's the way it is," he said.

That was on the wide bridge over the river. People passed and twisted to look closer, but did not stand because the breeze blew coldly from the river. Trams with lighted windows clanged past, with here half a man reading a paper or smoking, and there a girl staring straight ahead of her or perhaps patting her hair with deft fingers.

So the policeman grinned again and putting his fingers in his belt, turned and walked away.

Marty swung his grenades. Was he not Marty, an Irishman and a Dublin Fusilier? Son of no carey nor scab, but now and then the son of a seacook, and sometimes a son of a bitch, and always an oul' son of a gun. No sugarin' policeman would lay a hand on Marty. No dirty Jerry, nor snooping Boer, nor bloody Black and Tan. He'd banjax the whole issue, Marty would, all on his Barney Malone. But in the meanwhile, would you manage a pint, Marty? Would a duck swim, wha'? Willy is a bad fella. Right you are, oul' son, off we go for a loaf of Bolands.

Marty, letting out a shout, began to take his pint. A young man sat at the bar with his back to a partition, his raincoat unbuttoned, his hat on the back of his head. He had been talking to two men about music.

"I've been rehearsing for three solid hours," he said. "Bloody *Faust*. I've a thirst that a parish priest would sell his soul for."

"All the same," said the pavior, "*Faust* is a lovely opera."

"It's lovely," said the young man, "because it gives you a lovely thirst after rehearsing it for three solid hours."

"Mick and me," said the pavior, "used to play in the Trade Union band. We were thrown out for hocking the instruments when we were short for a few pints. We used to play selections from *Faust*."

"Rehearsing *Faust*," said Mick, "used to give us a lovely thirst too."

"What band was that?"

"Tell him what they called us, Tommy."

"They used to call us The Sufferin' Ducks," said the pavior reminiscently.

"It was very insultin' . . ." added Mick sadly.

Marty gave another yell out of him.

"That's Marty," the pavior said, "a harmless poor divil." He put a finger to his temple and twisted it significantly. His left eye winked.

"That was a terrible man once," said Mick, "that was a holy terror."

"Poor Marty," said the pavior.

"I remember the band during the big strike. We were marching down to a meeting at the docks. But when we got to Butt Bridge every bloody policeman in the country was there waiting for us."

"Drawn in a cordon across the street," put in Mick, "standing about ten deep with their batons in their hands and murder in their hearts."

"Your man Marty was the Bandmaster," the pavior continued, "and he gave us the order to halt. 'Where do you think you're going?' the Inspector came up and asked him. 'Down to a meeting,' said Marty. 'My men are drawn across there in front of you,' said the Inspector, 'and if you try to pass them they'll leave the lot of you for dead.' 'Will they?' said Marty, and the Inspector walked away. So Marty turned round to us. 'Strike it up boys,' he shouted, 'and forward on the double tap.' He waves his stick. 'Close your eyes, boys,' he says, 'and you won't feel the pain.'"

"It was slaughter, right enough," Mick commented.

"The police didn't like music," said the young man.

"They didn't like *our* music," Mick said sadly. "Marty had us playing *The Peeler and the Goat.*"

"That was Marty for you," concluded the pavior, turning to consult his pint.

Marty crouched staring in his corner, his head at an angle.

The curate, who knew Marty of an old date, nodded his head towards him and then winked at the pavior.

"We're off," said the pavior, "pension on Wednesday and pop goes the thinking cabinet."

"We're over the top all right," said Mick. "Next stop Blighty."

"What's wrong with him?" asked the young man, upset because Marty was staring at him with violence and hatred in his eyes.

"Shellshock," the pavior said. "I soldiered with Marty in France." Then he said loudly, "How's tricks, Marty oul' son?"

Marty continued to stare.

"He doesn't know you," Mick said. "Maybe he'll come round later."

Marty lived in the same house as the pavior, and a married sister who lived there looked after him. The pavior said Marty was a fine Soccer player once. He played for St. Patricks when they won the Leinster Senior Cup. That was against Sligo. They had a dinner after it in a hotel and then drove out to the Strawberry Beds on hacks and played melodeons and drank a lot of porter. But that was in Oul' God's time. In those days you could get a pint for twopence and any amount of cheese and biscuits for nothing. They were on the counter. You wouldn't see the like of that to-day.

"Them days is done," Mick declared. "You'd see white blackbirds before you'd see that again."

The pavior spat into the sawdust, and then scrubbed his heavy boot over it so that it made a trundling noise on the floor. The young man regarded Marty with curiosity. Marty, however, was watching the fellow with the machine gun. In France Marty had been going forward with his eye on that machine gun when the explosion blew him off his feet. He woke up blind, with a buzzing in his head. The blindness went away after a while but the buzzing remained intermittently. When it became bad Marty crouched and watched. Sometimes he would throw himself flat with a sudden wild movement, a loud obscenity. If he did this where there was concrete, Mrs. White, his married sister, had to get the enamel basin and bathe away the blood. Quite often he did it where there was concrete.

Marty took a grenade from the satchel, bit out the pin and swung his arm in a slow loop. When the flame and smoke subsided he saw in front of him the three shiny handles, like rifle nozzles protruding above three shoulders, which were used for pulling pints, and beyond them the glass mirror with its gilt advertisement for DWD potstill whiskey, the yellow pear of the electric bulb with its white shade, hanging plumb and without movement from the ceiling and the pavior's broad back. He heard also the hum of conversation and cars blowing horns now and then in the street. He found his pint almost finished. Would you have another Marty? He would because a bird never flew on one wing. He fetched out a bright silver shilling from his pocket.

> O Brian you've been drinking Brian O
> I know it by your winking Brian O . . .
> I took the Saxon shillin' for to do their dirty killin'
> The oul' sergeant found me willin'
>
> > Molly O.

So Marty gave his bright silver shilling to the curate and in return he received his pint and a few pence in change.

"All the same," the pavior said, "*Faust* is a fine opera."

"I remember it well," Mick said. "The Devil has a bit to do with it."

"Too much," agreed the young man.

"He sells his soul to the devil," continued the pavior thoughtfully, "for the sake of a slip of a girl."

"Shockin'," Mick said, "a bloody poor bargain."

"Many a man sold his soul for less, for a pint of porter or a piece of silver."

"That's the truth," Mick said.

"Yiz sold yer sowls for penny rolls and a cut of streaky bacon," quoted the pavior.

"No doubt about it," said Mick.

"Marty sold his soul for a shillin'," said the pavior with a finality which caused Mick, who did not quite follow, to shake his head in solemn agreement.

Marty gave his shilling. In the good days when he was young he would think himself well off with a shilling in his pocket of a Sunday morning.

One bright Sunday morning he left his mother's house in Patrick Street, his cap set gallantly, his shirt clean, his boots shining. Marty, young and vigorous, cocked an eye at the light cloud and the sun high up over the spire of the Cathedral. The clamouring bells shook the street, St. Audeon's, St. Patrick's, John's Lane and Christ Church, shouting and singing above the rattling cabs and the slaty cobbles, "Come and worship all ye true followers of Christ." He was going to Mass but he was thinking of other things. The bells he had grown up with made his head spin.

"Come and worship, Marty oul' son," said John's Lane. "Don't be dallying there with the sun warming your back and your eye giving the beck to the young girls with the feathers and the flowers in their hats."

"And them on their way to holy Mass too," said St. Audeon's. "Don't be hanging about there looking at the artificial sprays in the artificial ponds, and the dirty little urchins sailing paper boats in the close of St. Patrick's, the little desecrators of the Blessed Sabbath."

"He's dreaming about the medal he'll wear in his chain when they knock the stuffin' out of Sligo," said St. Patrick's. "He's thinking he might give it to Annie."

"Taking her out to the hollow in the park or maybe down the Shellybanks, God forgive him, that's what's occupying him."

As he walked, the hand which was in his pocket holding the shilling sweated so that he felt a moist circle in his palm.

"Come in, Marty," said John's Lane, "and pray a while for your soul. It could do with it. And pray for the souls of them that's gone—a summer's day is a long day."

Everybody harped at him.

"Marty Callaghan," his mother had said to him previously, "are you going to Mass at all?" He said he was ready, he had lashings of time. "It's on your knees in the church you should be now, not polishing your boots. If it was a football match you'd be in time, never fear." Marty whistled and winked at his young sister.

He stepped out of the sunlight into the porch of John's Lane, and taking off his cap and dipping his warm brown fingers in the holy water font, he crossed himself and sprinkled some at the door for the poor souls in purgatory. A large dim church cluttered with poor people. A warm place, the air shimmering with the tapering flame of candles and sour with the smell of devout bodies. He was in time for the first gospel and came out after the last, leaving the women to light their lamps to Saint Anne, patron of childing mothers, and the old men with rosary beads and yellow faces to keep watch against the thief who came by night. In the afternoon he walked with Annie through the Pigeon House fort where the soldiers practised firing, to the Shellybanks with their rough grasses which were sweet to lie in. They paddled in the shallow water and ate oranges, and Annie wore her blue dress. He asked her to marry him. Not immediately, he said, but soon. She said she didn't know really, she always thought she'd have liked a soldier. Dinny Andrews was a soldier and she thought it was a brave thing that, to be a soldier. He said he always thought she cared for him more than Dinny Andrews, and she said she did too, honest. Her eyes were blue and she laughed when she saw that he was moodily plucking at the grass. The grass cut his finger. She became very concerned, and made him bathe it in the salt water. After that she thought she might marry him. He went down to the men's place to swim, his heart singing, his lithe body pulsing with a new excitement. When he came back they bought oranges and sweets from the peddling women and ate them lying in the sandy grasses, watching the boats and the people who passed, laughing at the antics of little children and making love to one another.

In the evening he left her home, and that night he sat for a long time dreaming at the kitchen window, until it was midnight, and the bells of St. Patrick's having struck the hour, began as they always did at that hour to play a little tune, which stole quietly to him over streets and roof-tops.

Some nights later he told his father. He didn't know what to say to his mother. His father told her.

"Ellen," he said, "Marty's took the shillin'." He was sitting in a high armchair with his feet on the hob.

"I'm going to France, mother," Marty said, twiddling his cap in his hands. "I'm a soldier."

That was in the kitchen where the picture of Parnell hung between two bronze horses with warriors tilting at one another across the mantelpiece, and the speech of Robert Emmet stood framed on age-spotted parchment. "Let no man write my epitaph; for as no man who knows my motives dares now vindicate them, let not prejudice nor ignorance asperse them." Lovely round phrases which rolled in splendour from the mouth of his grandfather when he had a few jars in him.

One for the road and a bit of a song, Marty. Why not? It was a long time waiting for the war to be over. What would it be? Make it something Irish, was what they used to say to him.

Marty closed his eyes and turned his white face upwards. The sunken mouth opened and yellow molars stood up like cartridges. He sang *Danny Boy*. His voice was cracked and wobbly, like his broken body. His voice was a thing sewn and stitched together, wrapped like a ragged bandage about his song.

"There's a bit of a tune now for you," said Mick. Marty had his eyes fixed on the ceiling, displaying a scrawny neck where his Adam's apple ran to and fro between two deep ridges when he paused for breath after each line. The three of them turned to stare.

"He's putting his heart into it," said the pavior. They laughed.

> O Danny Boy, the pipes the pipes is callin'
> From glen to glen and down the mountain side,
> The summer's gone and all the flowers is dying
> 'Tis you must go, and so 'tis I must bide . . .

Two big tears rolled from Marty's eyes and lay on his cheeks on either side of his nose, matching the drop which now hung unmolested. The lower lids of both eyes, which sagged slightly outwards, were blood rimmed.

It was a sad song. Often his father had sung it at parties in their house in Patrick Street, because of course it was his father's song. It used to make his mother cry. It was always sad to think of the brave soldier marching off to the wars, leaving his father and his poor mother and the good kind people he loved. And his sweetheart too, who would wait for him until he came back.

> In sunshine or in shadow,
> And I will stand still waiting there for you.

But as like as not, he never came back.

A very sad, beautiful song, just like all the old songs. *When the fields are white with daisies I'll return* had been his mother's song. Marty had a face which made the barman exchange another nod and a wink with the three, who looked on happily, and a heart which was broken for love of poor dead days and their poor dead people, a spirit which groped back, always back with tearing and torture to his mother, God bless her, and his good father who drank come-day-go-day God-send-pay-day may the sod rest light on him, to Mick his brother who'd give the shirt off his back and Little One his sister who said give us a penny Marty there's a darlin' Marty for to buy seedy cake and he always gave it to her, and to other poor souls dead and gone this many a long day, may perpetual light shine upon them, may they rest in peace. Amen.

Marty stared at the ceiling. His mouth remained open. He found he was walking down by Dublin Castle and the clock striking midnight. A moon stared down at him from the cloud-racked sky. His grandfather stepped out from the shadows.

"Remember your oul' grandfather," said the voice, "I

cobbled boots for fifty years in Nash's Court. You used to laugh at me when my mouth was full of nails. You were only a dawny chisler then, Marty." He laughed again heartily at his grandfather, remembering the green baize apron and the cock of his hawky face over the boot. "An oul' cod," said Marty. He swung down the steep cobbles of Lord Edward Street.

"What about me," said a Callaghan with a greasy cloak, "that carried the keg of dynamite to the castle gate the time they pulled Kilwarden from his coach. They stuck twenty pitchforks in him to make sure he wouldn't remember who done it. Emmet was bloody annoyed, I can tell you."

"That was a wrong thing to do," Marty said, "even though he was only a Protestant." His boots rang on the cobbles. Under a guttering lamp another joined him. He was long and broad shouldered, but he had the hawky face.

"Did I ever tell you about 1534, Marty? I was keeping an eye on things after piling a bit of hay and me and Silken Thomas was having a drink together. 'Well, Fitzgerald,' says I, 'how's tricks?' 'Bad, Callaghan,' says he. 'They're after murdering the poor father. Do you see me sword of office?' 'I do,' I says. 'Well,' says he, 'as soon as I finish this mouthful I'm going straight over to the Abbey, and do you know what I'll do then?'

" 'I don't.'

" 'I'm going to take it off and throw it at the bloody Archbishop.'

" 'You'd be a foolish young man to do that,' I says.

" 'Foolish or not,' says he, 'that's the programme; and what's more, I hope it takes the bloody head off him, mitre an' all.' "

Marty yelled out loud at the idea of it. But a vague figure was following, whining and pulling at his sleeve. It had a death's head of a face, and a scrawny neck. "Fine talk," it said, "and fine men. But my potatoes withered in the ground and my youngest died with the green ooze of grass on his lips."

"They broke the house about my head," said another, "and the bailiff stood watching them and laughing."

"What odds; didn't you tie him to a gate afterwards and roast him over a fire?"

"We did—and when he died with God's mercy he went on roasting. I declare to God his carcase turned black as his heart."

Said the Inspector to him, "My men are drawn across in front of you, Marty, and if you try to pass them they'll leave the lot of you for dead."

But that was poor Erin for you, the tear and the smile in her eye.

He would meet Annie on some cool summer's evening out at the Strawberry Beds. In the distance someone would play a melodeon. Or once again perhaps in Phoenix Park on a day when the fields were white with daisies and golden with buttercups he'd return and the sky would be wide and blue above them, and the river a silver girdle far below. But it was a long time waiting for the war to be over.

The glass he was holding was flung violently to the ground. Mick and the barman jumped. "My Christ, Marty," said the barman, rushing out, "what the hell do you think you're doing?"

Marty swung both arms out wide.

"Atten-shun," he bawled.

"Attenshun nothing," said the barman, "that bloody glass cost eight pence." Marty screwed up his face and glared.

"Forward," he commanded. "At the double," he bawled.

"Leave him alone," said the pavior, "you might as well talk to the wall."

"He's over the top," averred Mick sadly.

"Breaking glasses is a new one. What the hell am I to do if everyone that has a pint can smash hell out of me glasses without an after you or a by your leave? It's all bloody fine."

"He couldn't help it, Joe," said the pavior soothingly.

"*Non compass mensit,*" explained Mick.

Marty, brushing aside the commotion, drew himself up and with dignity demanded a pint.

"There you are," the barman complained bitterly. "Now he has the bloody neck to ask me for a pint."

"Give it to him," they said, "he's all right now." Marty got his pint. He was talking to himself. They heard him arguing and swearing. Then he swung his grenades into position and marched out.

Tramp, tramp, tramp, went Marty the Dublin Fusilier. Pride in his heart and porter in his belly. The night hung mildly over the city, the streets were quiet, the dark houses stood up like tall sentries. Some taxi men, who were waiting for the theatres to close, stood smoking at the great gate of Stephen's Green. A faint scent of flowers hung in the air. Marty stood still at the corner. He stared ahead of him. Then he motioned with his arm. Then he stood still again. Then he howled an obscenity and began to lope forward. Now and then his arm swung in a wide loop. The noise of battle was about him. Once more in front of him was the fellow with the machine gun. His cheeks were grey and streaky with sweat and dust but his bared teeth were blinding white. Marty shouted out Tipperary, flung grenades, ran and stopped. But the machine gun continued to swing to and fro. When its black unwinking eye cocked itself wickedly in the centre of his regimental belt, Marty shouted and flung himself violently to the ground. His head struck on stone steps.

They said it was disgraceful that a man should get into such a condition. It was hard to know who was more to blame, the man himself or the publican who served him. A small knot had gathered when the pavior came along with Mick and the young man. The pavior knelt down and lifted him up. The pavior was the slightest bit tipsy.

"Marty oul' son," he said. Marty stirred.

"Come on, Marty, never say die. Old soldiers like you and me never die, Marty, we only fade away."

Marty murmured, "Attenshun."

"That's the spirit, Marty oul' son, that's the stuff to give the troops." He said to Mick, "For the love of God, will you take one side of him and don't stand there like a bloody statue."

Some money fell from his pocket as they lifted him, which Mick and the young man searched for while the pavior wiped blood from his face with his cap. There were traces of foam on Marty's mouth which he removed gently. "Have you his few ha'pence?" asked the pavior.

Mick, after peering around helplessly two or three times, said he didn't see any more. They helped him home. The spot where Marty had fallen was marked a little with blood, and in a corner by the iron railings where a little mound of dust had gathered winked a silver shilling. It lay waiting to be found by some passer-by with sharper eyesight than Mick. They took Marty up the broad carpetless stairs, their boots kicking each step and echoing as they struggled with their burden. Mrs. White, his sister, was in tears. "His poor face," she said when she saw him, "me poor Marty, what did they do to you?" And she got her green enamel basin and washed his face, and with her husband they put him to bed. Then she said there was tea waiting on the hob and they might as well have a cup.

"You're a good neighbour, God bless you," she said to the pavior. So they sat round drinking tea and saying Marty would be right as rain again to-morrow morning. But she kept saying, "What am I to do with him at all, at all? I can't be managing him for ever." And again she said, looking at her husband, "Wouldn't it be an unnatural thing to have him put away?" They talked until midnight in that way.

Marty lay in the little room. The window was open and let in the night noises, and the curtain stirred now and then faintly. The muscles of his hawky face twitched nervously, his mouth moved unceasingly. Sometimes his hands groped out for his satchel of grenades. St. Patrick's sounded midnight and the room reverberated. The bells died away. It was quiet and peaceful once more, with only the murmur of voices from the next room to break the silence. Marty slept. Then the bells of St. Patrick's, with their time-mellowed tongues, began to play a little tune.

THE WEB

WHEN the Black and Tan lorry left the strand road to swing instead towards the centre of the town, the Dummy was lounging at the corner house. All evening he had stood there in the mild warmth of the October sunlight, and though he was startled he did not move. But when the lorry passed close to him, his eyes narrowed and his head inclined slightly towards the wide strand on his left. He counted the turns. The engine slowed, revved, dropped again. It was going towards Freddie's house. By the time it stopped completely he was hammering loudly at one of the small cottages which faced the strand. There was no answer. He sucked his thumb and looked over his shoulder. About half a mile out in the centre of the pool-pocked sands two men were digging for bait. Their bent figures were diminutive with distance. Beyond them he could see the first foamy ridge of water and then the barracks at the extreme end of the breakwater towards which the lorry should normally have gone. He began to force the part-open window. Niall was standing at the foot of a disordered bed. He held a revolver which pointed at the window. The skin over his cheek bones and about his mouth was tight, and he held his gun steadily.

"I heard them," he said. "Tell Waxer."

The Dummy nodded and went swiftly through the hallway. In the kitchen he passed Mrs. Ryan. She had a loaf and a knife in her hands and her face was white. She followed him with wide eyes and moaned when his boots scraped on the wall of the small yard at the back.

When he returned she was with Niall in her husband's bedroom. It was disordered because Ryan had been cranky that evening and would let no one disturb him. His tea was cold and untouched beside his bed, and the buttered bread fouled with cigarette ash. Only his head was visible, a narrowed egg of a head and a face sunken and yellow.

"I'm a dyin' man, Waxer," he whined, "a dyin' man."

"We're all dyin' men," Waxer said. "You're not dying when it comes to finding your way to Tobin's of a Saturday."

He beckoned Niall and strode to the window.

"The stuff," he snapped without turning around. Niall bent over his father.

"Dad," he pleaded, "will you get up? Did you not hear them?"

"Am I ever hearin' anythin' else? They're goin' to the barracks."

"They're not," Niall said urgently. "They're goin' to Freddie's house."

His father shrank into an obstinate ball in the bed. His thin hands gripped the clothes tightly about his neck.

"What curse is over me?" he asked. "What possessed yiz to come in? There's no more guns goin' in here. I'm black and blue with the lumps under me mattress."

Niall gripped him by the shoulders and swung him to the

floor. While the mattress was rolled back he stood bent and shivering by his bed. His left hand clutched the neck of his nightshirt, and when a fit of coughing seized him, his right pulled the bottom downwards for decency.

"Waxer," he pleaded, "am I to spend me latter days lyin' on a bloody magazine?"

"Come on, come on," Waxer snorted. "Get the stuff out of that."

He leaned forward to peer through the window. There were lorries about the block and the room quivered sometimes with the trundling of them. Suddenly he stiffened.

"Dummy," he breathed, "get the manhole open."

Niall's mother crossed herself. The Dummy went out quickly to the back. The boots of soldiers grew loud on the pavement outside, while another lorry thundered in from the strand road. They were surrounding the house. Waxer motioned and Niall's mother followed them to the back yard.

"You'll have to put back the cover," Waxer said to her. "Lift it slowly and don't fuss. Then put your stool and the bathtub over it. Splash the water about as though you'd been washing."

Niall and she exchanged looks. She bit her lip.

"I will, Mr. Brannigan," she said, "I will."

Waxer let Niall and the Dummy down first. Then he followed nimbly. The sun lay warmly on the little yard and the bin in the corner cast a long shadow. Niall's shoulder brushed against the green ooze of the wall and the Dummy's nose wrinkled in disgust. Then the trap above was eased into position and the square of light narrowed and went out. They began to shuffle forward warily in the smelling darkness.

When the lorry pulled up outside Freddie's house the street was deserted except for a child with a white milk jug who

stood to watch. The old men who used to sit on the low window sills were gone, and their dogs and their gossip. From an
arc of wetness around a half-scrubbed doorstep, steam still rose
lightly, and here and there a furtive curtain moved. The child
went demurely up the street. She found Freddie with Phil
Tobin in the back bar.

"Well?" he said.

"The soldiers are at the house," she panted. "I ran."

"Did they see you?"

"No," she said, "they didn't mind me. I was fetchin' milk."

Phil Tobin was twisting his white apron with his hands.
He had fat stubby fingers. The apron was like a handkerchief
against the width of his stomach. Freddie put his hand on her
head.

"Good child," he said gently, "get the milk and bring it back
and say nothing."

He became anxious.

"Remember," he insisted quietly, "nothing."

She nodded and slipped out.

Phil tugged at his sleeve.

"For God's sake make a move," he said. "They'll be in on top
of us."

"That's right," Freddie answered. "They waste no time."

They picked their way through a tortuous passage and down
stone steps.

When they were in the cellar Phil said, "I knew it. Someone
informed."

"What makes you think that?"

"I'm no man's fool," said Phil Tobin.

"Unless we were seen, only yourself and the Ryans could
know."

"People can talk," said Phil.

Freddie glanced round at the barrels which littered the cellar, and at the grating which opened into the lane above. There was a mattress in the corner and a roll of blankets. He stooped and took out a revolver. Phil crumpled his apron in his hands. The apple-red of his lusty face was wrinkled and perturbed.

"I don't know in the name of God what prompted youse to come in," he declared.

"Orders," Freddie said, straightening. "Don't ask me why." He settled himself facing the door.

"You'd best get back to the shop," he said. "If they find me, tell them I came in through the grating."

Phil closed the door and went off with a nervous jangling of keys, and Freddie sat down to wait.

The soldiers searched his house. They swore at his mother because she would not answer them. They took his father, struggling, with them. Other houses were ransacked also. But when the night came and they were spread watchfully throughout the town, nothing had been found.

When they reached the mouth of the tunnel the sun was down and the smell of the sea stronger because it was night. From the fern-grown opening of the disused drain they could see the whole wide expanse of the strand; the lighthouse which stood beside the barracks at the extreme end of the breakwater, two miles of inkiness between, then the stringing of lamps along the coast road on their right, smears of blurred light through the misting rain. On the right, too, lay the Terrace and the house they had come from, Niall's house. The light was in his father's bedroom. He could single it out from all the lights along the strand road. When he was a child and night had overtaken his playing he had often walked to it in a straight line across the ebbed strand.

Niall stared for a long time at the light while they crouched in misery and felt the air damp about them.

"Somebody told," he said with sudden bitterness, "some rat."

"I know," Waxer said smoothly, "but who?"

"I don't know," Niall said; "someone."

He stared back into the darkness.

"They went to Freddie's house; I counted the turns."

"For all his smart talk," Waxer said, "Freddie is only a child; he wanted to be with his mother."

"He's got his bellyful now," Niall said. "You might as well talk to the wall." Waxer's mouth was closed tightly and his eyes looked to the right at nothing. He was thinking of several things at once.

But Niall's eyes moved restlessly, surveying the dripping walls, scanning the darkness.

"If they came to search here we're cornered. We can't get out."

Waxer smiled coldly. "We can get out the way we got in. You can always do that."

"No damn fear," Niall said, "not back through the house. I'm damned if we go that way."

"Who's giving orders?"

"To hell with orders," Niall said with heat. "That's one order you won't give." Waxer's mouth thinned.

"Who said so?" he asked evenly.

"I did. The mother is there and the da is a sick man, he's dyin'. If there was any trouble it would kill him."

Waxer smiled coldly. He sucked in his cheeks until the skin across the massive cheekbones was white. He let the matter rest.

"Until we know what's outside," he said, "we'll stay put."

The tunnel was dismally cold about them and the rain spun thinly across the dark sands. Sound travelled easily across the open space, but to-night the familiar noises were hushed. The darkness of narrow streets echoed now and then as a lorry moved off or changed its position, and that was all. Niall crouched and looked back along the tunnel which ran right under his home. He wondered if the soldiers had stayed in his house, and what his father and mother were doing. He had a long sallow face which at the moment was strained and apprehensive, and eyes that were at all times wide and lustrous. Opposite to him crouched the stocky figure of Waxer. It was Waxer who had brought both Niall and the Dummy into the movement. At the language-revival classes Niall had more aptitude than Waxer, but when it came to military action Waxer was officer. It was Waxer who had thought of exploring the almost forgotten tunnel and had arranged with H.Q. for using it as a dump. He was checking the barrel of the revolver which was his sole certificate for scholarship.

Niall watched the houselights on the shore go out one by one. He started at any unusual sound.

"All the same," he said later, "we shouldn't have come in. We were safe in the hills."

Waxer did not answer.

"Safer than here. It was bloody foolish to order four men . . ."

"Cut that out," Waxer said coldly. "Cut it out."

"I don't see . . ."

"Drop it," Waxer snarled.

The Dummy looked up mildly. He had taken possession of the bomb and was playing idly with it. Though he was young enough to wear knickerbockers, the legs beneath his black stockings were muscular. His lips were turned up and slightly parted, as though smiling at his thoughts.

"When you've knocked off four officers," Waxer said grimly, "you're safe nowhere." He spat into the darkness. He looked at the Dummy and then lay back against the tunnel-wall once more.

"Yer a good soldier," he said drily, "you don't answer back."

The Dummy grinned and continued to play idly with the bomb. A long time later, when they were chilled and cramped and everyone had forgotten the context, Waxer said:

". . . Nowhere."

When Ryan walked up the plots the following morning there were fewer men than usual. They looked at him sympathetically and let him pass when he showed little inclination to linger. Nothing more had happened during the night. He had been wakened early by his wife. It was a clear morning of sunshine and light white clouds. The sun was on the front of the house and had filled the bedroom as he raised himself on his elbow to lean over the breakfast tray.

"Nuthin' happened?" he had asked, screwing up his eyes.

She glanced covertly at the soldier who sat in the window.

"What could happen," she had said indifferently, "and them miles away."

"That's right," he said, "of course."

He grunted uneasily.

"It's bright out, d'yeh think?"

"Like a summer's morning—thank God. You could take your walk."

"I will," he decided, "I'll take a turn down to the Bakery." It was his habit when Saturday was fine. He would walk down to the Bakery for his pension and then up the strand road for a pipe and a chat.

He showed improvement, the men sometimes said to him. It pleased him and made him feel better. "It's the dry weather," he would say; "the doctor says I should go to a sanatorium. It'd cure me, he says."

But that morning he went by without a word. He shuffled moodily past them and stopped some distance away at the strand wall. They saw him huddle with his hands deep in his pockets, staring and staring at the bright pools which flashed in the wake of the tide.

One of the men said, "The soldiers were in the house all night. Isn't it a queer thing they should let him out?" and another, "He's waitin' for the band to play. They can't be hidin' forever."

Phil was with Freddie on and off during the day. There was little doing in the shop. The soldiers were still in the streets and people did not go out without necessity. When he was taking away the remains of Freddie's dinner he said, "I sent that note you gave me. The youngster took it."

"Good," Freddie said. "If an answer comes, bring it immediately. Was there anything else?"

"Ryan was out and about."

"He goes down for the pension," Freddie said.

Phil said meaningly, "The soldiers are in his house."

"What about it?" Freddie asked irritably.

"Nothing," Phil answered mildly, "except that it's funny they should let him out."

Freddie ran his hands quickly through his hair.

He said, "No man would spit on his own son." There were dark circles under his eyes and his face was pinched. His eyes were quick and nervous.

"Men do queer things, especially sick men."

Freddie shook his head. He looked around at the dust-encrusted walls, at the barrels tilted about the floor and the cobwebs which stretched like threadbare rags across every corner of the low ceiling. He began to pace restlessly.

"I wish to God I could get away from here," he said at last. Then: "Will Ryan be here to-night?"

"Always on a Saturday."

"Watch him," Freddie said, "and if an answer comes, let me know." The keys jangled and the beat of feet on the stone stairway dwindled once more into silence. There was still light in the cellar, and on the grating above loud feet clanged on occasion and passed. But there were long silences, during which he crouched in a corner from which he could command the door, smoking cigarettes, watching a spider spreading its dexterous web between two barrels. It stopped occasionally as though to stare at him. Now and then he blew smoke from his cigarette in a gentle stream towards the web. This would send it scurrying out of sight. His eyes narrowed as he considered the spider. Once he laughed suddenly. Then his mood changed. He broke the web in sudden disgust. It retired altogether for a time, but later came back and began to spin once more. It was inexorable. The streets grew hushed as the light failed and the cellar echoed not at all. The dust, smelling more strongly, foretold rain.

It began that night when the men in Tobin's were beginning to glance at the yellow-faced clock. At first, but for the diminutive drops which flecked the windows, it was hardly noticeable. But later it grew fierce. They sat and heard the wind rise and the rain sweeping over streets and little houses, over limp ropes and hanging nets and the dreary stretches of sand. There was little conversation. A stranger stood for a time at the bar, had some words with Phil, and when the rain was beginning, left. Ryan was there also. He sat nearer the right-hand end of the counter and lingered over his drinks. His overcoat was too big for him and pieces of fluff clung to it because of his habit of throwing it on the foot of the bed. He spoke to no one except Phil. He stared miserably into space and tapped absently at his chin with a bony finger.

Whenever Phil stood before him he took out a purse and fumbled awkwardly as he paid.

"It's a poor night," he said and looked down at his drink.

"It is," Phil answered, "for a man on his keeping."

When the men were leaving, Phil went down and stood before him with his hands resting on the counter. He looked down steadily at him.

"The sergeant is in the snug," Phil said levelly. "They were round at the house looking for you."

"Lookin'?" Ryan repeated.

"They want to question you."

"Question Phil. They'd have your soul damned into hell with their questions. They'd have you tormented." He looked right and left quickly. He reached out with bony fingers to caress Phil's arm.

"Phil," he asked, "have you word of Niall, do you know where they are?"

"Where?"

"I'm askin' you, Phil, you that knew them." He leaned forward. "Are they in the tunnel—I know there's a tunnel. Are they there?"

"You seem to know more than I do," Phil said.

Ryan looked down at his drink. His face was old and yellow-lined like a rotten apple. His eyes, like Niall's, swam with

odd lustre, but they were sunken and peeped from a distance.

"I don't, Phil," he breathed, "I know nuthin'. I didn't even know they were coming back. But if they're in the tunnel it's not safe. I have word, I—I heard them talking, last night in the bedroom . . ."

"You're keepin' the sergeant," said Phil coldly.

"Maybe I am, Phil, but I swear before God Naill is a good boy and I played fair by him. He'd tell you that. I reared him and I put the clothes on his back. I worked when I should have been at home in me bed. The doctor said a sanatorium would cure me, but it meant money and I couldn't see him hungry. There was nuthin' he had that didn't come from me." Phil's eyes mocked him.

"I wouldn't harm a hair on his head," he said almost to himself, "nor let others do it." A hand was laid on his shoulder. He turned around.

"There's a couple of questions I'd like to ask," said the sergeant, "so finish your business . . ."

Phil came in with the note and held the candle so that Freddie could read. The flame quivered and the grease dripped over and stung his fingers. The shadows retreated from the flame. They huddled in a ring about the two of them. Outside the rain ran in rivulets down channels, and the soldiers, scattered at their stations throughout the town, crouched miserably and swore. They looked up at the skies and wished for something to happen. Freddie stuck the note into the flame. They watched in silence while it burned.

"I've got to go," Freddie said. "I've to find the rest."

"You'll find no one to-night, are you mad?"

"I'll find them all right. Put out the candle and help me to raise the grating."

"I won't," Phil said backing away. "Why can't you bide your time?"

"Quickly," Freddie said, "there isn't any time."

He listened acutely. There was no sound but the monotonous beat of the rain. He snuffed the candle and caught Phil by the arm. They began to build a pyramid of crates directly under the grating. When they had finished Phil's face ran with sweat. They eased up the gate cautiously. There was no creaking on account of the rain. Freddie let himself through. He crouched for a moment to listen. Phil stood by while the gate was lowered. Freddie signed to him, straightened quickly, and strode away.

He went casually through the darkened town, his shoulders hunched and his head down against the rain. Nobody passed; the streets were deserted; lorries stood here and there by the side of the road, vacant and dead beneath the swollen skies, like derelict ships.

But when he reached the strand there were soldiers at intervals along the wall. One was so near that he could hear the crunch of his boots and the irritable clank of equipment. He stopped dead. He was intensely aware of the web that had been built around him, a web which for months had been growing about him, a web he must break from or perish in. The spider was spinning. His eyes narrowed as each sense became suddenly sharpened. After a while he dropped to his knees and made with painful slowness towards the wall.

They crouched in the darkness, each withdrawn into himself, so that they were three beings, three isolated points of life in a vast solitude. The great ferns which cluttered the mouth of the tunnel were swaying and dripping, but when the wind dropped they could hear sounds on the beach, lost sounds that were lonely like eternity. Niall shuddered and when a fit of coughing seized him he would bury his mouth in his cap in order to stifle it. When shots rang out he licked his lips and glanced through the darkness at Waxer and the Dummy.

His face was grey. The smell of the tunnel and the strain of waiting had made him sick. His limbs were cramped and stiff with waiting. He was fascinated when either of the others moved or betrayed signs of life.

"Who the hell are they firing at?" he asked, his voice rising.

"Maybe they're jittery," said Waxer, "shootin' their shadows."

"We should have shifted last night, Waxer. We could have made it."

"We waited for word."

"How could they send it?"

"If I know anythin' about it," said Waxer, "they'll find a way. They won't let the dump go."

"If Freddie was caught . . ."

"Hush," Waxer said, "we've got to listen."

Niall hunched miserably. He squirmed and became uneasy, chafing at his helplessness. He drew his knees up to his chin, then stretched them full length; he turned on one side. Then he shifted again, rubbed a cramped leg, crouched once more over his knees. Sometimes he sighed. But Waxer and the Dummy sat unmoved.

They were silent until the Dummy half rose and grunted.

"What?" Waxer snapped, and Niall jerked forward with his hand going automatically to his pocket. The Dummy jabbed his thumb towards the strand. They listened. Somebody slid down the embankment some distance away. A tin can clinked and then rolled noisily, and shots rang out.

"Christ," Niall said, panicking. He scrambled forward on his hands and knees towards the tunnel entrance.

"Back," Waxer growled, "you bloody fool, back towards the house."

The Dummy sat rigid, his mouth and eyes narrow lines. Niall still went forward.

"Them's orders," Waxer hissed, "and put that revolver away."

"Go to hell," Niall said. Waxer swore and pounced. Feet slithered on the embankment below and someone fell forward into the tunnel. Waxer flung sideways and came to grips.

"Who is it?" he snarled, and his fingers slipped swiftly upwards.

"Me," Freddie said simply.

Waxer loosened his grip. He felt his hands sticky.

"You're hit."

"Left shoulder," Freddie said. "They caught me when I'd crossed the wall."

"We'd better shift, is it bad?"

"I can't say," Freddie answered. "I had a message from Cassidy. I burned it and came straight."

"Good work," Waxer said. He looked quickly behind him and then back at Freddie.

"Do you know how things are?"

But Freddie had slumped back against the wall. He was quite young, almost as young as the Dummy. His face beneath the shock of dark curls was pale. It was scratched and streaked with sand where he had fallen when the bullets struck him. His nose still bled slightly. Waxer and the Dummy looked on while Niall wiped away the sand with his handkerchief.

"See to his shoulder," said Waxer, "and bring him round. We don't want him on our hands."

"I don't want to strip his shoulder," Naill answered. "I think it might be dangerous in this atmosphere."

"That's right," grumbled Waxer, "do nuthin' you're told." But he made no move himself. He lay back and watched while Niall bent in silence over Freddie. The Dummy shaded a small torch with his body.

"He's bleeding like hell," Niall whispered in sudden terror. "Why don't you do something?"

"Wake him up," demanded Waxer, "I want to know all I can."

Niall shook Freddie.

"Freddie," he pleaded, "Freddie, don't sleep now. Do you hear me? We've got to get away from here."

Freddie murmured and twisted his head from side to side.

"What's he say?"

"He's wandering," Naill answered, frightened. "Something about spiders . . ."

Waxer grunted.

After a while Freddie sighed with his whole body and opened his eyes. Waxer leaned forward.

"There's a first-aid kit in th ebend by the dump," he said to Naill. "You'll get bandages there." He nodded to the Dummy. "Show him," he added.

When they had gone he spoke to Freddie. "Now," he said.

"Cassidy sent word by Phil. I was in the cellar . . . watching the . . . They're coming for the dump to-night."

"Are you sure of that?"

"Intelligence says so. You've to lay a fuse if you can and then get out. They'll have a car outside the Ivy Church . . ."

"The Ivy Church," Waxer said ironically, "that's a bloody good one."

"Someone informed . . ." Freddie added.

"Who?" demanded Waxer.

Freddie moved weakly and looked straight at Waxer. He hesitated.

"Niall's father," he said.

Waxer slid forward to the mouth of the tunnel. Here and there on the strand lights moved. They jerked in nervous bars in the blackness. He thought they were coming nearer, but very slowly. When he got back Niall was leaning once more over Freddie.

"They're coming," he said.

Niall looked quickly over his shoulder. Then he went on with his bandaging.

"Do you know who spilt?" he asked between clenched teeth. Freddie looked queerly at him.

"No, Niall," he said, "I don't know."

There was a short silence during which the Dummy's eyes turned with half-understanding from Waxer to Freddie. Freddie looked away and Waxer's eyes focussed on the ground between his feet.

"We've got to move quickly," Waxer said after a pause. "Can you make it, Freddie?"

Freddie nodded.

"Very well. We'll go back by the house."

Niall bit his lip. He seemed on the point of tears.

"Waxer," he said, "it'll kill me da, it'll be the death of him."

Waxer swore.

"Waxer," Niall appealed. "Supposin' they're still in the yard . . ."

"It's dark. If we go out shooting there's a chance. You and I will go first. Then while we cover them the Dummy will help Freddie through. Is that clear?"

Niall bowed his head. They nodded. There were noises from

the strand as the ring drew nearer. They could feel the ring tightening on them. Waxer gestured with the revolver.

"All right," he said, "move."

He betrayed no emotion.

They followed, crouched, through the darkness. Once Freddie fell, and the Dummy helped him to his feet. They passed the opening of a tunnel on their right. It was at right angles to the main tunnel but had been blocked up about twenty yards from the opening. It contained the dump. There were bandages scattered here and there from Niall's searching. The Dummy paused but Waxer said, "There isn't time."

When they were crouching under the manhole which opened into Niall's back yard there were loud reports and shots ricochetted through the tunnel.

"Quick," Waxer said.

Niall went to his side and pressed his hands against the manhole. He took the strain with his wrists. Then he rose slowly and bent his arms. Waxer grunted and they pushed violently. The cover lifted with the sudden pressure. It went skidding across the yard. Then the rain was wet on their faces.

Waxer fired into the darkness, covering the scullery door and the opposite wall. Freddie gained the yard but the bin tripped him and he fell. He rose painfully, firing while Niall and Waxer broke for the back wall. "Freddie," Niall screamed, beckoning, "Freddie." But Freddie did not attempt the wall. He turned instead towards the house. After a while he was alone in the yard. He was dimly aware of lights and a kitchen table, and further away, like a long dark tunnel, the hallway and an open door. Beyond the door were soldiers. They opened fire. He shouted and lunged savagely forward. They closed around the hall door. They shot solidly until he reeled against the bedroom door. It swung inwards and he pitched headlong into the room. He moaned and breathed painfully . . .

The Dummy lay back along the tunnel. They had followed him, forcing him slowly yard by yard back to the dump. He was not quite dead. But though the bomb had rolled away from him, the pin which he had withdrawn was still clutched in his hand. It was intensely dark. In front of him and behind him, at about twenty yards' distance, were bars of light and cautiously approaching feet. . . .

When Freddie opened his eyes there was no one besides Ryan in the room. At first Freddie did not see him. He was watching the spider. It fascinated him. It crept across the floor, now stopping, now moving forward. It grew giant-like and after diminished; it became three spiders, and then ten, all marching or floating in a serried line. Sometimes they wavered and dissolved, sometimes all were spinning furiously. It became one again. Then slowly he was aware of a voice from the bed, an incoherent mumbling. He saw a head above the bedclothes and a thin hand which clutched rosary beads. He stretched his arm along the floor towards the revolver.

He said, "Why did you do it?"

The hand tightened.

Ryan sat up. He looked in terror at Freddie. He had been crying. He shuddered and said, "I didn't know youse were comin' back—I swear—youse told me nuthin'—what are you doin' with the gun?"

"It's not for you," Freddie answered, "it's for the spider."

Ryan saw no spider. His eyes searched. His jaw fell open.

"Why?"

The spider, Freddie knew, had caused the trouble. The spider had made a web. It must be found. He raised himself painfully on his elbow.

Ryan yelled in alarm.

"Freddie—for the love of God—I didn't know youse were coming back. I only knew about the dump. There wasn't badness in that, not just about the dump."

"Why . . ." Freddie breathed.

He hardly knew he asked the question. He had found the spider. It was crawling slowly over the bedclothes towards the beads and the hand. As Ryan sank back against the pillow Freddie raised the revolver. He levelled at the spider, lost sight of it, then levelled again.

Ryan moaned and said, "How could I know youse were coming back?"

Then he closed his eyes. His voice, tired and almost inaudible, murmured, "I wanted the money. I wanted it for a sanatorium."

Freddie fired twice at the spider. It disappeared. He stared and saw the stain of blood growing on the sheets. Then suddenly his elbow gave under him and he pitched forward. His eyes were still open. When the explosion shook the room a moment later he neither moved nor heard.

But Waxer and Niall heard. They lay flat in the rain and the darkness. The little garden shuddered with the noise of lorries and about them they could feel the inexorable closing-in of the search. They looked sideways at one another.

Two blocks away, aeons away, looming over low roofs and intersecting walls, rose the Ivy Church.

JANEY MARY

WHEN Janey Mary turned the corner into Nicholas Street that morning, she leaned wearily against a shopfront to rest. Her small head was bowed and the hair which was so nondescript and unclean covered her face. Her small hands gripped one another for warmth across the faded bodice of her frock. Around the corner lay Canning Cottages with their tiny, frost gleaming gardens, and gates that were noisy and freezing to touch. She had tried each of them in turn. Her timid knock was well known to the people who lived in Canning Cottages. That morning some of them said, "It's that little 'Carthy one, never mind opening. Twice in the last week she's been around —it's too much of a good thing." Those who did answer her had been dour. They poked cross and harassed faces around half-open doors. Tell her mammie, they said, it's at school she should have her, and not out worrying poor people the likes of them. They had the mouths of their own to feed and the bellies of their own to fill, and God knows that took doing.

The school was in Nicholas Street and children with satchels were already passing. Occasionally Janey Mary could see a

few paper books peeping from an open flap, and beside them
a child's lunch and a bottle of milk. In the schoolroom was a
scrawled and incomprehensible blackboard, and rows of staring faces which sniggered when Janey Mary was stupid in her
answers.

Sometimes Father Benedict would visit the school. He asked
questions in Catechism and gave the children sweets. He was
a huge man who had more intuition than intellect, more genuine affection for children than for learning. One day he found
Janey Mary sitting by herself in the back desk. She felt him,
giant-like above her, bending over her. Some wrapped sweets
were put on her desk.

"And what's your name, little girl?"

"Janey Mary 'Carthy, Father."

"I'm Father Benedict of the Augustinians. Where do you
live?" Father Benedict had pushed his way and shoved his way
until he was sitting in the desk beside her. Quite suddenly
Janey Mary had felt safe and warm. She said easily, "I lives
in Canning Cottages."

He talked to her while the teacher continued self-consciously
with her lesson.

"So, your daddy works in the meat factory?"

"No, Father, my daddy's dead."

Father Benedict nodded and patted her shoulder. "You and
I must be better friends, Janey," he said. "We must tell your
mammie to send you to school more often."

"Yes, Father."

"Because we must see more of one another, mustn't we?"

"Yes, Father."

"Would you always come?"

"I'd like to come, Father."

Father Benedict had talked with her for some time like that, the pair of them crushed clumsily in the desk and their heads close together. When he was leaving he gave her more sweets. Later the teacher took them from her as a punishment and gave them out again as little prizes for neatness.

She thought of Father Benedict until an old beggar who was passing said to her, "Are you whingin', child? Is there anything up with you?"

She lifted her head and looked stupidly at him, her mouth open and her eyes quite dry. He was a humpbacked man with broken boots and a bulbous nose. The street about him was a moving forest of feet; the stolid tread of workmen and the pious shuffle of middle-aged women on their way from Mass.

"You look a bit shook, kid," he said. "Are you after taking a turn?"

"No, mister," she said, wondering. "I'm only going for to look for bread at St. Nicholas's. My mammie told me."

"Your mammie left it a bit late. They'll be going in for to pray." As though awakened by his words, the bell of the Augustinian Friary rang three times. It rang out with long, resounding strokes across the quivering street, and people paused to uncover their heads and to bless themselves.

Janey Mary looked up quickly. The steeple of the church rose clear and gleaming above the tall houses, and the golden slimness of its cross raced swiftly against the blue and gold of the sky.

Her mother had said, "Look till you find, my lady, and you won't lose your labour. This is the day of the Blessed Bread and if you get it nowhere else they'll be giving it out at St. Nicholas's."

She turned suddenly and ran quickly up the length of the

street. But when she reached the priory the doors were closed and the waiting queue had broken into small knots. She stopped uncertainly and stared for some time.

The priests, the people said, had gone in to pray. They would be back in an hour.

She was glad to turn homewards. She was tired and her bare feet moved reluctantly on the ice-cold pavement. Johnny might have been given some bread on his round with the sticks, or her mother might have had some hidden away. Her mother sometimes did that so that Janey Mary would try very hard to get some.

Picking her way amongst the debris-littered wasteland upon which houses had once stood, she watched her shadow bobbing and growing with the uneven rippling of the ground. The light of the wintry sun rested wanly on everything and the sky was dizzily blue and fluffed a little with white cloud. There were rust-eaten tin cans lying neglected on the waste, and fragments of coloured delf which she could have gathered to play chaneys had she had the time. The children often went there to play shop; they marked out their pitches with a file of pebbles in the form of an open square. When Janey Mary stood in one of the squares for a moment she was no longer Janey Mary. The wasteland became a busy street and the tracery of pebbles glittering stores. Her face would grow grave. It was that serene gravity of a child at play. But when she stepped out of the magic square she was again Janey Mary, a Janey Mary who was cold and hungry and whose mother was waiting impatiently for bread that had not been found.

"There was none," she said, looking up at her mother's face. "Nobody would give it and the man said the priests wouldn't be back for an hour." She looked around hopefully as she spoke, but there were only a few crumbs on the table. They

littered its grease-fouled and flower-patterned covering. An enamel jug stood in the centre and about it the slopped ugliness of used cups. Now that she was home she realised how endless the morning's trudging had been. She realised how every door had been closed against her. Her mother's voice rose.

"Then you can do without. Are you after looking at all, you little trollop? Two hours to go the length of the street and around to the holy priests, and us all in a wakeness with the hunger. And Johnny going out with the sticks and him famished but for the little bit I had left away. Are you after looking atall?"

The enamel of the jug was broken in three places. The breaks were spidery, like the blobs of ink which used to fall so dishearteningly on her copy books. Down the side of each cup clung the yellow residue of dribbled tea. The whole table shifted suddenly and went back again, and her mother's voice seemed far away. Janey Mary wanted to sit down.

"Gallivanting," her mother said, "off gallivanting with your pals. I'll gallivant you. But you can go back again. There's nothing in the house. Back with you to the priests' house and wait like any Christian for what's going. And take the bag with you. You won't do a hand's turn till you do that."

Janey Mary stood with her hands clasped in front of her and looked up at her mother. The thought of going back again filled her with misery.

"I asked," she said. "I asked everywhere."

"Then you can ask again," said her mother. "You can ask till you find," and swung away. Janey Mary went wearily to the corner to fetch the bag. The kitchen trembled and became dark when she bent to pick it up. As she went out of the door her mother said:

"Put a bit of hurry on yourself and don't be slinging. It's certain you'll never die with the beating of your heart. The world and its wife would get something and mine 'd be left."

Once more she was out in the ancient crookedness of streets, picking her way amidst the trundling of wheels and the countless feet. Tiny and lost beneath the steepness of houses, she went slowly, her bare feet dragging and dirty. At this hour the shops in Nicholas Street were crowded with women who haggled over half pennies. White-coated assistants leaned quickly over marble-topped counters with heads cocked to one side and pencils raised in readiness, or dashed from counters to shelves and back again, banging things on the scales and then licking pencil stubs while they frowned over figures. Sometimes Janey Mary used to stand and watch them, but now she went by without interest. When a tram went grinding past her, her lips trembled, and though the rails after it and before it gleamed in the sunlight, it was a pale cold gleaming. There was no friendly heat in the sunlight. There was nothing friendly. There were only trundling trams and the tramp of feet, and once again the slim cross on the spire of St. Nicholas's.

On the Feast of the Blessed Bread it was the custom of the priests to erect a wooden counter on the high steps before the door of the priory. Here two of the brothers stood to watch the forming of the queue. Janey Mary looked hard through the veil which blurred occasionally in front of her eyes, but could catch no sign of Father Benedict. No bread had yet appeared though the queue was growing. She took her place and kept close to the wall. In near the wall she found it easier to hold her position. It was very cold at first, but after a while more people came and the air grew warmer. They came, as she had known they would, with baskets and shawls, with torn shopping bags and ragged coats, and gathered thickly about her.

There were men there too, old pensioners and men who had not worked for years.

"There won't be much going," they said. "There was a shocking crowd here this morning."

"Take your bloody hour," they said. "Who d'you think you're pushing?"

"Aisy, aisy, mind the chisler."

They talked like that for a long time. At first they argued furiously with one another. But later they became dour with impatience. They shuffled uncomfortably. They spat frequently and heaved long sighs.

After a while it became frightening to be in there so close to the wall, to be so small that everyone towered over you. Janey Mary felt weak and wanted to get out. When she glanced sideways or ahead of her she could see nothing but tightly packed bodies, and when she looked down there were feet, but no ground. She tried to look upwards, but could not. An hour passed before Father Benedict appeared on the steps.

"Father Benedict, God bless him," they said. "It'll be coming soon when he's here."

Janey Mary was lifted clear off the ground by the movement of the crowd and lost her place. Now she was behind a stoop-backed man with a threadbare coat and heavily nailed boots. His collar was flaked and greasy with dandruff and his coat was foul smelling, but it was the boots which held Janey Mary's attention. They clattered unsteadily on the pavement very close to her bare feet. There were diamond-shaped nails in double rings about the heels of them. She bent to keep her eyes fixed on the boots and wriggled to avoid them. Her attention became fixed on them. To a man near her she said, "I want to get out, mister, let me get out," but even if he had heard her he could not have helped her now. She tried to attract attention, but they had forgotten her. They kept telling one another over and over again what each of them already knew.

"It's coming," they said, pressing forward, "it's coming." And after a while the murmuring changed and the queue surged.

"Look," they shouted, "it's here."

Janey Mary was lifted once more. Once more her feet were clear of the ground and her breathing stifled by the pressure of those around her. She was in danger now and clawed whimpering at the dandruff flaked collar. Through a whirl of arms and shoulders she had a view of Father Benedict, his broad shoulders tall and firm above the press of bodies. She tried to call out to him.

"The chisler," someone said, noticing. "For God's sake quit pushing. Look at the chisler." A man threw out his hand to grip her, but a movement of the crowd twisted him suddenly aside. She saw his hand grabbing futilely to her left. As the crowd parted she began to slip.

"Father Benedict," she called faintly, "Father Benedict." Then the man in front stumbled and the nailed boots crushed down heavily on her feet.

When her eyes opened again she was on the sofa in the visitors' parlour. Father Benedict and one of the lay brothers were bending over her. Someone had put a rug about her. An electric fire glowed warmly against the opposite wall, and over it hung a gold-framed picture of the Sacred Heart. Her feet felt numb and heavy and the picture swam before her eyes. But it was warm in the parlour and the morning's searching was over. Then she remembered the bread and her mother's words. She moved suddenly, but when she tried to speak her

ears were filled with noise. The lay brother had turned
to Father Benedict.

"You were very quick," he was saying. "Is she badly hurt?"

Father Benedict, answering him, said in a strange voice.

"Only her feet . . . You can see the print of the nails . . ."

THE EAGLES AND
THE TRUMPETS

WHEN the girl crossed from the library, the square was
bathed in August sunshine. The folk from the outlying
areas who had left their horses and carts tethered about the
patriotic monument in the centre were still in the shops, and
the old trees which lined either side emphasised the stillness
of the morning. She went down a corridor in the Commercial
Hotel and turned left into the bar. She hardly noticed its
quaintness, the odd layout of the tables, its leather chairs in
angles and corners, the long low window which looked out on
the dairy yard at the back. After six years in the town she was
only aware of its limitations. But the commercial traveller
startled her. She had not expected to find anyone there so early.
He raised his eyes and when he had stared at her gloomily for
a moment, he asked, "Looking for Cissy?"

One of the things she had never got used to was this easy
familiarity of the country town. But she accepted it. One either
accepted or became a crank.

"No," she answered, "Miss O'Halloran."

"You won't see her," he said. "It's the first Friday. She goes to the altar and has her breakfast late." He had a glass of whiskey in front of him and a bottle of Bass. He gulped half the whiskey and then added, "I'll ring the bell for you."

"Thank you."

His greyish face with its protruding upper lip was vaguely familiar. Probably she had passed him many times in her six years without paying much attention. Now she merely wondered about his black tie. She heard the bell ringing remotely and after a moment Cissy appeared. The girl said:

"I really wanted Miss O'Halloran. It's a room for a gentleman to-night." She hesitated. Then reluctantly she added, "Mr. Sweeney." As she had expected, Cissy betrayed immediate curiosity.

"Not Mr. Sweeney that stayed here last autumn?"

"Yes. He hopes to get in on the afternoon bus."

Cissy said she would ask Miss O'Halloran. When she had gone to enquire, the girl turned her back on the traveller and pretended interest in an advertisement for whiskey which featured two dogs, one with a pheasant in its mouth. The voice from behind her asked.

"Boyfriend?"

She had expected something like that. Without turning she said, "You're very curious."

"Sorry. I didn't mean that. I don't give a damn. Do you drink?"

"No, thank you."

"I was going to offer you something better than a drink. Good advice." The girl stiffened. She was the town librarian, not a chambermaid. Then she relaxed and almost smiled.

"If you ever do," the voice added sadly, "don't mix the grain with the grape. That's what happened to me last night."

Cissy returned and said Mr. Sweeney could have room seven. Miss O'Halloran was delighted. Mr. Sweeney had been such a nice young man. Her eye caught the traveller and she frowned.

"Mr. Cassidy," she said pertly, "Miss O'Halloran says your breakfast's ready."

The traveller looked at her with distaste. He finished his whiskey and indicated with a nod of his head the glass of Bass which he had taken in his hand.

"Tell Miss O'Halloran I'm having my breakfast," he said. But Cissy was admiring the new dress.

"You certainly look pretty," she said enviously.

"Prettiest girl in town," the traveller added for emphasis.

The girl flushed. Cissy winked and said, "Last night he told me I was."

"Did I?" the traveller said, finishing his Bass with a grimace of disgust. "I must have been drunk."

On the first Friday of every month, precisely at 11.45, the chief clerk put on his bowler hat, hung his umbrella on his arm and left to spend the rest of the day inspecting the firm's branch office. It was one of the few habits of the chief clerk which the office staff approved. It meant that for the rest of the evening they could do more or less as they pleased. Sweeney, who had been watching the monthly ceremony from the public counter with unusual interest, turned around to find Higgins at his elbow.

"You're wanted," he was told.

"Who?"

"Our mutual musketeer—Ellis. He's in his office."

That was a joke. It meant Ellis was in the storeroom at the
top of the building. Part of the duties assigned to Ellis was the
filing away of forms and documents. The firm kept them for
twenty-five years, after which they were burned. Ellis spent
interminable periods in the storeroom, away from supervision
and interference. It was a much-coveted position. Sweeney,
disturbed in his day-dreaming, frowned at Higgins and said:

"Why the hell can't he come down and see me?" It was his
habit to grumble. He hated the stairs up to the storeroom and
he hated the storeroom. He disliked most of the staff, especially
the few who were attending night school classes for accountancy and secretarial management in order to get on in the job.
Put into the firm at 19 years of age because it was a good, safe,
comfortable job, with a pension scheme and adequate indemnity against absences due to ill-health, he realised now at 26
that there was no indemnity against the boredom, no contributory scheme which would save his manhood from rotting
silently inside him among the ledgers and the comptometer
machines. From nine to five he decayed among the serried
desks with their paper baskets and their telephones, and from
five onwards there was the picture house, occasional women,
and drink when there was money for it.

The storeroom was a sort of paper tomb, with tiers of forms
and documents in dusty bundles, which exhaled a musty odour.
He found Ellis making tea. A paper covered book had been
flung to one side. On the cover he could make out the words
Selected Poems, but not whose they were. He was handed a
cup with a chocolate biscuit in the saucer.

"Sit down," Ellis commanded.

Sweeney, surprised at the luxury of the chocolate biscuit,
held it up and inspected it with raised eyebrows.

Ellis offered milk and sugar.

"I pinched them out of Miss Bouncing's drawers," he said deliberately.

Sweeney, secure in the knowledge that the chief clerk was already on his way across town, munched the biscuit contentedly and looked down into the street. It was filled with sunshine. Almost level with his eyes, the coloured flags on the roof of a cinema lay limp and unmoving, while down below three charwomen were scrubbing the entrance steps. He took another biscuit and heard Ellis saying conversationally, "I suppose you're looking forward to your week-end in the country."

The question dovetailed unnoticed in Sweeney's thought.

"I've been wanting to get back there since last autumn. I told you there was a girl . . ."

"With curly eyes and bright blue hair."

"Never mind her eyes and her hair. I've tried to get down to see her twice but it didn't come off. The first time you and I drank the money—the time Dacey got married. The second, I didn't get it saved in time. But I'm going to-day. I've just drawn the six quid out of Miss Bouncing's holiday club."

"What bus are you getting?"

"The half past two. His nibs has gone off so I can slip out."

"I see," Ellis said pensively.

"I want you to sign me out at five."

They had done things like that for one another before. Turning to face him, Ellis said, "Is there a later bus?"

"Yes. At half past eight. But why?"

"It's . . . well, it's a favour," Ellis said uncertainly. With sinking heart Sweeney guessed at what was coming.

"Go on," he invited reluctantly.

"I'm in trouble," Ellis said. "The old man was away this past two weeks and I hocked his typewriter. Now the sister's

'phoned me to tip me off he's coming home at half past two.
They only got word after breakfast. If I don't slip out and re-
deem it there'll be stinking murder. You know the set-up at
home."

Sweeney did. He was aware that the Ellis household had
its complications.

"I can give it back to you at 6 o'clock," Ellis prompted.

"Did you try Higgins?" Sweeney suggested hopefully.

"He hasn't got it. He told me not to ask you but I'm desperate. There's none of the others I can ask."

"How much do you need?"

"Four quid would do me—I have two."

Sweeney took the four pound notes from his wallet and
handed them over. They were fresh and stiff. Miss Bouncing
had been to the bank. Ellis took them and said:

"You'll get this back. Honest. Byrne of the Prudential is to
meet me in Slattery's at six. He owes me a fiver."

Still looking at the limp flags on the opposite roof Sweeney
suggested, "Supposing he doesn't turn up."

"Don't worry," Ellis answered him. "He will. He promised
me on his bended knees."

After a pause he diffidently added, "I'm eternally grateful . . ."

Sweeney saw the week-end he had been aching for receding
like most of his other dreams into a realm of tantalising un-
certainty.

"Forget it," he said.

II

Sweeney, who was standing at the public counter, looked up
at the clock and found it was half past two. Behind him many

of the desks were empty. Some were at lunch, others were taking advantage of the chief clerk's absence. It only meant that
telephones were left to ring longer than usual. To his right,
defying the grime and the odd angles of the windows, a streak
of sunlight slanted across the office and lit up about two square
feet of the counter. Sweeney stretched his hand towards it and
saw the sandy hairs on the back leap suddenly into gleaming
points. He withdrew it shyly, hoping nobody had seen him.
Then he forgot the office and thought instead of the country
town, the square with its patriotic statue, the trees which lined
it, the girl he had met on that autumn day while he was walking along through the woods. Sweeney had very little time for
romantic notions about love and women. Seven years knocking
about with Ellis and Higgins had convinced him that Romance,
like good luck, was on the side of the rich. It preferred to ride
around in motor cars and flourished most where the drinks
were short and expensive. But meeting this strange girl among
the trees had disturbed him. Groping automatically for the
plausible excuse, he had walked towards her with a pleasur-
able feeling of alertness and wariness.

"This path," he said to her, "does it lead me back to the
town?" and waited with anxiety for the effect. He saw her assessing him quickly. Then she smiled.

"It does," she said, "provided you walk in the right direction."

He pretended surprise. Then after a moment's hesitation he
asked if he might walk back with her. He was staying in the
town, he explained, and was still finding his way about. As
they walked together he found out she was the town librarian,
and later, when they had met two or three times and accepted
one another, that she was bored to death with the town. He
told her about being dissatisfied too, about the office and its

futility, about having too little money. One evening when they were leaning across a bridge some distance from the town, it seemed appropriate to talk rather solemnly about life. The wind rippled the brown water which reflected the fading colours of the sky. He said:

"I think I could be happy here. It's slow and quiet. You don't break your neck getting somewhere and then sit down to read the paper when you've got there. You don't have twenty or thirty people ahead of you every morning and evening—all queuing to sign a clock."

"You can be happy anywhere or bored anywhere. It depends on knowing what you want."

"That's it," he said, "but how do you find out? I never have. I only know what I don't want."

"Money—perhaps?"

"Not money really. Although it has its points. It doesn't make life any bigger though, does it? I mean look at most of the people who have it."

"Dignity?" she suggested quietly.

The word startled him. He looked at her and found she was quite serious. He wondered if one searched hard enough, could something be found to be dignified about. He smiled.

"Do you mean an umbrella and a bowler hat?"

He knew that was not what she meant at all, but he wanted her to say more.

"No," she said, "I mean to have a conviction about something. About the work you do or the life you lead."

"Have you?" he asked.

She was gazing very solemnly at the water, the breeze now and then lifting back the hair from her face.

"No," she murmured. She said it almost to herself. He slipped his arm about her. When she made no resistance he kissed her.

"I'm wondering why I didn't do that before," he said when they were finished.

"Do you . . . usually?" she asked.

He said earnestly, "For a moment I was afraid."

"Of me?"

"No. Afraid of spoiling everything. Have I?"

She smiled at him and shook her head.

At five they closed their ledgers and pushed in the buttons which locked the filing cabinets. One after the other they signed the clock which automatically stamped the time when they pulled the handle. The street outside was hardly less airless than the office, the pavements threw back the dust-smelling August heat. Sweeney, waiting for Higgins and Ellis at the first corner, felt the sun drawing a circle of sweat about his shirt collar and thought wistfully of green fields and roadside pubs. By now the half-past-two bus would have finished its journey. The other two joined him and they walked together by the river wall, picking their way through the evening crowds. The tea-hour rush was beginning. Sweeney found the heat and the noise of buses intolerable. A girl in a light cotton frock with long hair and prominent breasts brushed close to them. Higgins whistled and said earnestly, "Honest to God, chaps. It's not fair. Not on a hot evening."

"They're rubber," Ellis offered with contempt.

"Rubber bedamned."

"It's a fact," Ellis insisted. "I know her. She hangs them up on the bedpost at night."

They talked knowledgeably and argumentatively about falsies until they reached Slattery's lounge. Then, while Ellis began to tell them in detail how he had smuggled the type-writer back into his father's study, Sweeney sat back with relief and tasted his whiskey. A drink was always welcome after a day in the office, even to hold the glass in his hand and lie back against his chair gave him a feeling of escape. Hope was never quite dead if he had money enough for that. But this evening it wasn't quite the same. He had hoped to have his first drink in some city pub on his way to the bus, a quick drink while he changed one of his new pound notes and savoured the adventure of the journey before him, a long ride with money in his pocket along green hedged roads, broken by pleasant half hours in occasional country pubs. When Higgins and Ellis had bought their rounds he called again. Whenever the door of the lounge opened he looked up hopefully. At last he indicated the clock and said to Ellis, "Your friend should be here."

"Don't worry," Ellis assured him, "he's all right. He'll turn up." Then he lifted his drink and added, "Well—here's to the country."

"The country," Higgins sighed. "To-morrow to fresh fiends and pastors new."

"I hope so," Sweeney said. He contrived to say it as though it didn't really matter, but watching Ellis and Higgins he saw they were both getting uneasy. In an effort to keep things moving Higgins asked, "What sort of a place is it?"

"A square with a statue in it and trees," Sweeney said. "A hotel that's fairly reasonable. Free fishing if you get on the right side of the Guards. You wouldn't think much of it."

"No sea—no nice girls in bathing dresses. No big hotel with its own band."

"Samuel Higgins," Ellis commented. "The man who broke the bank at Monte Carlo."

"I like a holiday to be a real holiday," Higgins said stoutly. "Stay up all night and sleep all day. I like sophistication, nice girls and smart hotels. Soft lights and glamour and sin. Lovely sin. It's worth saving for."

"We must write it across the doorway of the office," Sweeney said.

"What?"

"Sin Is Worth Saving For."

It had occurred to him that it was what half of them did. They cut down on cigarettes and scrounged a few pounds for their Post Office Savings account or Miss Bouncing's Holiday Club so that they could spend a fortnight of the year in search of what they enthusiastically looked upon as sin. For him sin abounded in the dusty places of the office, in his sweat of fear when the morning clock told him he was late again, in the obsequious answer to the official question, in the impulse which reduced him to pawing the hot and willing typist who passed him on the deserted stairs.

"I don't have to save for sin," he commented finally.

"Oh—I know," Higgins said, misunderstanding him. "The tennis club is all right. So are the golf links on Bank Holiday. But it's nicer where you're not known."

"View Three," Ellis interjected. "Higgins the hen butcher."

"Last year there was a terrific woman who got soft on me because I told her I was a commercial pilot. The rest of the chaps backed me up by calling me Captain Higgins. I could have had anything I wanted."

"Didn't you?"

"Well," Higgins said, in a tone which suggested it was a bit early in the night for the intimate details. "More or less." Then they consulted the clock again.

"It doesn't look as though our friend is coming," Sweeney said.

"We'll give him 'til seven," Ellis said. "Then we'll try for him in Mulligan's or round in the Stag's Head."

III

The girl watched the arrival of the bus from the entrance to the hotel. As the first passenger stepped off she smiled and moved forward. She hovered uncertainly. Some men went past her into the bar of the Commercial, the conductor took luggage from the top, the driver stepped down from his cabin and lit a cigarette. Townspeople came forward too, some with parcels to be delivered to the next town, some to take parcels sent to them from the city. He was not among the passengers who remained. The girl, aware of her new summer frock, her long white gloves, the unnecessary handbag, stepped back against the wall and bumped into the traveller.

"No boyfriend," he said.

She noticed he had shaved. His eyes were no longer bloodshot. But the sun emphasised the grey colour of his face with its sad wrinkles and its protruding upper lip. As the crowd dispersed he leaned up against the wall beside her.

"I had a sleep," he said. "Nothing like sleep. It knits up the ravelled sleeve of care. Who said that, I wonder?"

"Shakespeare," she said.

"Of course," he said, "I might have guessed it was Shakespeare."

"He said a lot of things."

"More than his prayers," the traveller conceded. Then he looked up at the sun and winced.

"God's sunlight," he said unhappily. "It hurts me."

"Why don't you go in out of it?" she suggested coldly.

"I've orders to collect. I'm two days behind. Do you like the sun?"

"It depends."

"Depends with me too. Depends on the night before. Mostly I like the shade. It's cool and it's easy on the eyes. Sleep and the shade. Did Shakespeare say anything about that, I wonder?"

"Not anything that occurs to me." She wished to God he would go away.

"He should then," the traveller insisted. "What's Shakespeare for, if he didn't say anything about sleep and the shade?"

At another time she might have been sorry for him, for his protruding lip, his ashen face, the remote landscape of sorrow which lay behind his slow eyes. But she had her own disappointment. She wanted to go into some quiet place and weep. The sun was too strong and the noise of the awakened square too unsettling. "Let's talk about Shakespeare some other time," she suggested. He smiled sadly at the note of dismissal.

"It's a date," he said. She saw him shuffling away under the cool trees.

When they left Slattery's they tried Mulligan's and in the Stag's Head Higgins said he could eat a farmer's arse, so they had sandwiches. The others had ham and beef but Sweeney took egg because it was Friday. There was a dogged streak of religion in him which was scrupulous about things like that. Even in his worst bouts of despair he still could observe the prescribed forms. They were precarious footholds which he hesitated to destroy and by which he might eventually drag himself out of the pit. After the Stag's Head Ellis thought of the Oval.

"It's one of his houses," he said. "We should have tried it before. What's the next bus?"

"Half eight."

"Is it the last?"

"The last and ultimate bus. Aston's Quay at half past eight. Let's forget about it."

"It's only eight o'clock. We might make it."

"You're spoiling my drink."

"You're spoiling mine too," Higgins said, "all this fluting around."

"You see. You're spoiling Higgins' drink too."

"But I feel a louser about this."

"Good," Higgins said pleasantly. "Ellis discovers the truth about himself."

"Shut up," Ellis said.

He dragged them across the city again.

The evening was cooler. Over the western reaches of the Liffey barred clouds made the sky alternate with streaks of blue and gold. Steeples and tall houses staggered upwards and caught the glowing colours. There was no sign of Byrne in the Oval. They had a drink while the clock moved round until it was twenty minutes to nine.

"I shouldn't have asked you," Ellis said with genuine remorse.

"That's what I told you," Higgins said. "I told you not to ask him."

"Byrne is an arch louser," Ellis said bitterly. "I never thought he'd let me down."

"You should know Byrne by now," Higgins said. "He has medals for it."

"But I was in trouble. And you both know the set-up at home. Christ if the old man found out about the type-writer . . ."

"Look," Sweeney said, "the bus is gone. If I don't mind, why should you? Go and buy me a drink." But they found they hadn't enough money left between them, so they went around to the Scotch House where Higgins knew the manager and could borrow a pound.

IV

Near the end of his holiday he had taken her to a big hotel at a seaside resort. It was twenty miles by road from the little town, but a world away in its sophistication. They both cycled. Dinner was late and the management liked to encourage dress. A long drive led up to the imposing entrance. They came to it cool and fresh from the sea, their wet swimming togs knotted about the handlebars. It was growing twilight and he could still remember the rustle of piled leaves under the wheels of their bicycles. A long stone balustrade rose from the gravelled terrace. There was an imposing ponderousness of stone and high turrets.

"Glenawling Castle," he said admiringly. She let her eyes travel from the large and shiny cars to the flag-mast some hundreds of feet up in the dusky air.

"Comrade Sweeney," she breathed, "cast your sweaty night-cap in the air."

They walked on thick carpet across a foyer which smelled of rich cigar smoke. Dinner was a long, solemn ritual. They had two half bottles of wine, white for her, red for himself. When he had poured she looked at both gleaming glasses and said happily:

"Isn't it beautiful? I mean the colours." He found her more astoundingly beautiful than either the gleaming red or the white.

"You are," he said. "Good God, you are." She laughed happily at his intensity. At tables about them young people were in the minority. Glenawling Castle catered to a notable extent for the more elevated members of the hierarchy, Monsignors and Bishops who took a little time off from the affairs of the Church to play sober games of golf and drink discreet glasses of brandy. There were elderly business men with their wives, occasional and devastatingly bored daughters.

After dinner they walked in the grounds. The light had faded from the sky above them but far out to sea an afterflow remained. From the terrace they heard the sound of breakers on the beach below and could smell the strong, autumn smell of the sea. They listened for some time. He took her hand and said: "Happy?"

She nodded and squeezed his fingers lightly.

"Are you?"

"No," he said. "I'm sad."

"Why sad?"

"For the old Bishops and the Monsignors and the business men with their bridge-playing wives."

They both laughed. Then she shivered suddenly in the cool breeze and they went inside again to explore further. They investigated a room in which elderly men played billiards in their shirt sleeves, and another in which the elderly women sat at cards. In a large lounge old ladies knitted, while in deep chairs an occasional Bishop read somnolently from a priestly book. Feeling young and a little bit out of place, they went into the bar which adjoined the ballroom. There were younger people here. He called for drinks and asked her why she frowned.

"This is expensive for you," she said. She took a pound note from her bag and left it on the table.

"Let's spend this on the drinks," she suggested.

"All of it?"

She nodded gravely. He grinned suddenly and gave it to the attendant.

"Pin that on your chest," he said, "and clock up the damage until it's gone."

The attendant looked hard at the note. His disapproval was silent but unmistakable.

"It's a good one," Sweeney assured him. "I made it myself."

They alternated between the ballroom and the bar. In the bar she laughed a lot at the things he said, but in the ballroom they danced more or less silently. They were dancing when he first acknowledged the thought which had been hovering between them.

"I've only two days left."

"One, darling."

"To-morrow and Saturday."

"It's to-morrow already," she said, looking at her watch. Now that it was said it was unavoidably necessary to talk about it.

"It's only about two hours by bus," he said. "I can get down to see you sometimes. There'll be week-ends."

"You won't though," she said sadly.

"Who's going to stop me?"

"You think you will now but you won't. A holiday is a holiday. It comes to an end and you go home and then you forget."

They walked through the foyer which was deserted now. The elderly ladies had retired to bed, and so had the somnolent churchmen with their priestly books.

"I won't forget," he said when they were once again on the terrace. "I want you too much."

The leaves rustled again under their wheels, the autumn air raced past their faces coldly.

"That's what I mean," she said simply. "It's bad wanting anything too much." Her voice came anonymously from the darkness beside him.

"Why?" he asked.

Their cycle lamps were two bars of light in a vast tunnel of darkness. Sometimes a hedge gleamed green in the light or a tree arched over them with mighty and gesticulating limbs.

"Because you never get it," she answered solemnly.

V

Sweeney, looking through the smoke from Higgins and Ellis to the heavily built man whom he did not like, frowned and tried to remember what public house he was in. They had been in so many and had drunk so much. He was at that stage of drunkenness where his thoughts required an immense tug of his will to keep them concentrated. Whenever he succumbed to the temptation to close his eyes he saw them wandering and grazing at a remote distance from him, small white sheep in a landscape of black hills and valleys. The evening had been a pursuit of something which he felt now he would never catch up with, a succession of calls on some mysterious person who had always left a minute before. It had been of some importance, whatever he had been chasing, but for the moment he had forgotten why. Taking the heavily built man whom he didn't like as a focal point, he gradually pieced together the surroundings until they assumed first a vague familiarity and then a positive identity. It was the Crystal. He relaxed, but not too much, for fear of the woolly annihilation that might follow, and found Higgins and the heavily built man swopping stories. He remembered that they had been swopping stories for a long time. The heavily built man was a friend of Higgins'. He had an advertising agency and talked about the golf club and poker and his new car. He had two daughters—clever as hell. He knew the Variety Girls and had a fund of smutty stories. He told them several times they must come and meet the boys. "Let's leave this hole," he said several times, "and I'll run you out to the golf club. No bother." But someone began a new story. And besides, Sweeney didn't want to go. Every time he looked at the man with his neat suit and his moustache, his expensively fancy waistcoat and the pin in his tie, he was tempted to get up and walk away. But for Higgins' sake he remained and listened. Higgins was telling a story about a commercial traveller who married a hotel keeper's daughter in a small country town. The traveller had a protruding upper lip while the daughter, Higgins said, had a protruding lower lip. Like this, Higgins said. Then he said look here he couldn't tell the story if they wouldn't pay attention to him.

"This'll be good boys," the man said, "this will be rich. I think I know this one. Go on."

But Higgins said hell no they must look at his face. It was a story and they had to watch his face or they'd miss the point.

"Christ no," Ellis said, "not your face."

Sweeney silently echoed the remark, not because he really objected to Higgins' face but because it was difficult to focus it in one piece.

Well, Higgins said, they could all sugar off, he was going to tell the story and shag the lot of them.

"Now, now," the man said "we're all friends here. No unpleasantness and no bickering, what?"

"Well," Higgins continued, "the father of the bride had a mouth which twisted to the left and the mother's mouth, funny enough, twisted to the right. So on the bridal night the pair went to bed in the hotel which, of course, was a very small place, and when the time came to get down to certain important carry-on, the nature of which would readily suggest itself to the assembled company; no need to elaborate, the commercial traveller tried to blow out the candle. He held it level with his mouth but, of course, on account of the protruding upper lip his breath went down in the direction of his chin and the candle remained lit." Higgins stuck out his lip and demonstrated for their benefit the traveller's peculiar difficulty. "'Alice,' said the traveller to his bride, 'I'll have to ask you to do this.' So her nibs had a go and, of course, with the protruding lower lip, her breath went up towards her nose, and lo and behold the candle was still lighting." Again Higgins demonstrated. "'There's nothing for it, John, but call my father,' says she. So the oul' fella is summoned and he has a go. But with his lips twisted to the left the breath goes back over his shoulder and the candle is still lighting away. 'Dammit, this has me bet,' says the father, 'I'll have to call your mother,' and after a passable delay the oul' wan appears on the scene but, of course, same thing happens, her breath goes out over her right shoulder this time, and there the four of them stand in their nightshirts looking at the candle and wondering what the hell will they do next. So they send out for the schoolmaster, and the schoolmaster comes in and they explain their difficulty and ask him for his assistance and 'certainly,' he says, 'it's a great pleasure.' And with that he wets his finger and thumb and pinches the wick and, of course, the candle goes out." Higgins wet his finger and thumb and demonstrated on an imaginary candle. "Then the father looks at the other three and shakes his head. 'Begod,' says he, 'did youse ever see the likes of that, isn't education a wonderful thing?' " The heavily built man guffawed and asserted immediately that he could cap that. It was a story about a commercial traveller too. But as he was about to start they began to call closing time and he said again that they must all come out to the golf club and meet the boys.

"Really," he said, "you'll enjoy the boys. I'll run you out in the car."

"Who's game?" Higgins asked.

Ellis looked at Sweeney and waited. Sweeney looked at the heavily built man and decided he didn't dislike him after all. He hated him.

"Not me," he said, "I don't want any shagging golf clubs."

"I don't care for your friend's tone," the man began, his face reddening.

"And I don't like new cars," Sweeney interrupted, rising to his feet.

"Look here," the heavily built man said threateningly. Ellis and Higgins asked the stout man not to mind him.

"Especially new cars driven by fat bastards with fancy waistcoats," Sweeney insisted. He saw Ellis and Higgins moving in between him and the other man. They looked surprised and that annoyed him further. But to hit him, he would have had to push his way through them and it would take so much effort that he decided it was hardly worth it after all. So he changed his mind. But he turned around as he went out.

"With fancy pins in their ties," he concluded. People moved out of his way.

They picked him up twenty minutes later at the corner. He was gazing into the window of a tobacconist shop. He was wondering now why he had behaved like that. He had a desire to lean his forehead against the glass. It looked so cool. There was a lonely ache inside him. He barely looked round at them.

"You got back quick," Sweeney said.

"Oh cut it out," Ellis said, "you know we wouldn't go without you."

"I hate fat bastards with fancy pins," Sweeney explained. But he was beginning to feel it was a bit inadequate.

"After all," Higgins said, "he was a friend of mine. You might have thought of that."

"Sugar you and your friends."

Higgins flushed and said, "Thanks, I'll remember that."

Pain gathered like a ball inside Sweeney and he said with intensity, "You can remember what you sugaring well like."

"Look," Ellis said, "cut it out—the pair of you."

"He insulted my friend."

"View four," Ellis said, "Higgins the Imperious."

"And I'll be obliged if you'll cut out this View two View three View four stuff . . ."

"Come on," Ellis said wearily, "kiss and make up. What we all need is another drink."

It seemed a sensible suggestion. They addressed themselves to the delicate business of figuring out the most likely speakeasy.

VI

The last bus stayed for twenty minutes or so and then chugged out towards remoter hamlets and lonelier roads, leaving the square full of shadows in the August evening, dark under the trees, grey in the open spaces about the statue. The air felt thick and warm, the darkness of the sky was relieved here and there with yellow and green patches. To the girl there was a strange finality about the departure of the bus, as though all the inhabitants had boarded it on some impulse which would leave the square empty forever. She decided to have coffee, not in the Commercial where Cissy was bound to ask questions, but in the more formal atmosphere of the Imperial. She had hoped to be alone, and frowned when she met the traveller in the hallway. He said:

"Well, well. Now we can have our chat about Shakespeare." She noticed something she had not observed earlier—a small piece of newspaper stuck on the side of his cheek where he had cut himself shaving. For some reason it made her want to laugh. She could see too that he was quite prepared to be rebuffed and guessed his philosophy about such things. Resignation and defeat were his familiars.

"I see you've changed your location," she said, in a voice which indicated how little it mattered.

"So have you."

"I was going to have coffee."

"We can't talk Shakespeare over coffee," he invited. "Have a drink with me instead."

"I wonder should I. I really don't know you," she answered coolly.

"If it comes to that," he said philosophically, "who does?"

They went into the lounge. The lounge in the Imperial paid attention to contemporary ideas. There were tubular tables and chairs, a half moon of a bar with tube lighting which provided plenty of colour but not enough light. The drink was a little dearer, the beer, on such evenings in August, a little too warm. He raised his glass to her.

"I'm sorry about the boyfriend," he said. She put down her glass deliberately.

"I'd rather you didn't say things like that," she said. "It's not particularly entertaining. I'm not Cissy from the Commercial, you know."

"Sorry," he said repentantly, "I meant no harm. It was just for talk's sake."

"Then let's talk about you. Did you pick up your two days' orders?"

"No," he said sadly, "I'm afraid I didn't. I'm afraid I'm not much of a commercial traveller. I'm really a potter."

"Potter?"

"Yes. I potter around from this place to that."

She noticed the heavy upper lip quivering and gathered that he was laughing. Then he said:

"That's a little joke I've used hundreds of times. It amuses me because I made it up myself."

"Do you often do that?"

"I try, but I'm not much good at it. I thought of that one, God knows how many years ago, when things began to slip and I was in bed in the dark in some little room in some cheap hotel. Do you ever feel frightened in a strange room?"

"I'm not often in strange rooms."

"I am. All my life I've been. When I put out the light I can never remember where the door is. I suppose that's what makes me a pretty poor specimen of a traveller."

"So you thought of a joke."

"Yes."

"But why?"

"It helps. Sometimes when you feel like that a joke has more comfort than a prayer."

She saw what he meant and felt some surprise.

"Well," she prompted. "Why do you travel?"

"It was my father's profession too. He was one of the old stock. A bit stiff and ceremonious. And respected of course. In those days they didn't have to shoot a line. They had dignity. First they left their umbrella and hat in the hall stand. Then there was some polite conversation. A piece of information from the city. A glass of sherry and a biscuit. Now you've got to talk like hell and drive like hell. I suppose he trained me the wrong way."

He indicated her glass.

"You'll have another?" he asked.

She looked again at his face and made her decision. She was not quite sure what it would involve, but she knew it was necessary to her to see it out.

"I think I will," she said.

He asked her if she liked her work but she was not anxious to discuss herself at all. She admitted she was bored. After their third drink he asked her if she would care to drive out with him to Glenawling Castle. There were not likely to be people there who knew them and besides, there would be dancing. She hesitated.

"I know what you're thinking," he said, "but you needn't worry. I'm no he-man." She thought it funny that that was not what had occurred to her at all. Then he smiled and added:

"With this lip of mine I don't get much opportunity to practice."

They got into the car which took them up the hill from the square and over the stone bridge with its brown stream. The traveller looked around at her.

"You're a pretty girl," he said warmly, "prettiest I've met."

She said coolly, "Prettier than your wife?"

"My wife is dead."

She glanced involuntarily at the black tie.

"Yes," he said, "a month ago." He waited. "Does that shock you?" he asked.

"I'm afraid it does."

"It needn't," he said. "We were married for eighteen years, and for fifteen of that she was in a lunatic asylum. I didn't visit her this past eight or nine years. They said it was better. I haven't danced for years either. Do you think I shouldn't?"

"No," she said after a pause. "I think it might do you good. You might get over being afraid of strange rooms."

"At forty-five?" he asked quietly.

His question kept the girl silent. She looked out at the light racing along the hedges, the gleaming leaves, the arching of trees.

VII

They eventually got into Annie's place. It was one of a row of tall and tottering Georgian houses. Ellis knew the right knock and was regarded with professional affection by the ex-boxer who kept the door. They went in the dark up a rickety stairs to a room which was full of cigarette smoke. They had to drink out of cups, since the girls and not the liquor were the nominal attraction. There was some vague tradition that Annie was entitled to serve meals too, but to ask for one was to run the risk of being thrown out by the ex-boxer. The smell of the whiskey in his cup made Sweeney shiver. He had had whiskey early in the evening and after it plenty of beer. Experience had taught him that taking whiskey at this stage was a grave mistake. But no long drinks were available and one had to drink. Ellis noted his silence.

"How are you feeling?" he asked with friendly solicitude.

"Like the Chinese maiden?" Higgins suggested amiably and tickled the plump girl who was sitting on his knee.

"No," Sweeney said, "like the cockle man."

"I know," Higgins said. "Like the cockle man when the tide came in. We all appreciate the position of that most unfortunate gentleman." He tickled the plump girl again. "Don't we, Maisie?"

Maisie, who belonged to the establishment, giggled.

"You're a terrible hard root," she said admiringly.

There were about a dozen customers in the place. One group had unearthed an old-fashioned gramophone complete with sound horn and were trying out the records. They quarrelled about whose turn it was to wind it and laughed uproariously at the thin nasal voices and the age of the records. Sweeney was noted to be morose and again Ellis had an attack of conscience.

"I feel a louser," Ellis said.

"Look," Sweeney said, "I told you to forget it."

"Only for me you could be down the country by now."

"Only for me you could be out at the golf club," Sweeney said, "drinking with the best spivs in the country. You might even have got in the way of marrying one of their daughters."

The gramophone was asking a trumpeter what he was sounding now.

"God," Maisie said, "my grandfather used to sing that. At a party or when he'd a few jars aboard. I can just see him."

"My God. Where?" Higgins asked in mock alarm.

"In my head—Smarty," Maisie said. "I can see him as if it was yesterday. Trumpet-eer what are yew sounding now—Is it the cawl I'm seeking?"

They looked in amazement at Maisie who had burst so suddenly into song. She stopped just as suddenly and gave a sigh of warm and genuine affection. "It has hairs on it right enough —that thing," she commented.

"What thing?" Higgins enquired salaciously and was rewarded with another giggle and a playful slap from Maisie.

"Maisie darling," Ellis appealed, "will you take Higgins away to some quiet place?"

"Yes," Sweeney said. "Bury his head in your bosom." Maisie laughed and said to Higgins, "Come on, sweetheart. I want to ask them to put that thing on the gramophone again." As they went away the thought struck Sweeney that Mary Magdalene might have looked and talked like that and he remembered something which Ellis had quoted to him earlier in the week. He waited for a lull among the gramophone playing group and leaned forward. He said, groping vaguely:

"Last week you quoted me something, a thing about the baptism of Christ . . . I mean a poem about a painting of the baptism of Christ . . . do you remember what I mean?"

"I think I do," Ellis said. Then quickly and without punctuation he began to rattle off a verse. "A painter of the Umbrian School Designed upon a gesso ground The nimbus of the baptised God The wilderness is cracked and browned."

"That's it," Sweeney said. "Go on."

Ellis looked surprised. But when he found Sweeney was not trying to make a fool of him he clasped the cup tightly with both hands and leaned across the table. He moved it rhythmically in a small wet circle and repeated the previous verse. Then he continued with half-closed eyes.

> "But through the waters pale and thin
> Still shine the unoffending feet . . ."

"The unoffending feet," Sweeney repeated, almost to himself. "That's what I wanted. Christ—that's beautiful."

But the gramophone rasped out again and the moment of quietness and awareness inside him was shattered to bits. Higgins came with three cups which he left down with a bang on the table.

"Refreshment," he said, "Annie's own. At much personal inconvenience."

Sweeney looked up at him. He had been on the point of touching something and it had been knocked violently away from him. That always happened. The cups and the dirty tables, the people drunk about the gramophone, the girls and the cigarette smoke and the laughter seemed to twist and tangle themselves into a spinning globe which shot forward and shattered about him. A new record whirled raspingly on the gramophone for a moment before a tinny voice gave out the next song.

> Have you got another girl at home
> Like Susie,
> Just another little girl upon the family tree?
> If you've got another girl at home
> Like Susie . . .

But the voice suddenly lost heartiness and pitch and dwindled into a lugubrious grovelling in the bass.

"Somebody wind the bloody thing," Ellis screamed. Somebody did so without bothering to lift off the pick-up arm. The voice was propelled into a nerve-jarring ascent from chaos to pitch and brightness. Once again the composite globe spun towards him. Sweeney held his head in his hands and groaned. When he closed his eyes he was locked in a smelling cellar with vermin and excrement on the floor, a cellar in which he groped and slithered. Nausea tautened his stomach and sent the saliva churning in his mouth. He rose unsteadily.

"What is it?" Ellis asked.

"Sick," he mumbled. "Filthy sick."

They left Higgins behind and went down into the street. Tenements with wide open doors yawned a decayed and malodorous breath, and around the corner the river between grimy walls was burdened with the incoming tide. Sweeney leaned over the wall.

"Go ahead," Ellis said.

"I can't."

"Stick your fingers down your throat."

Sweeney did so and puked. He trembled. Another spasm gripped him. Ellis, who was holding him, saw a gull swimming over to investigate this new offering.

"It's an ill wind . . ." he said aloud.

"What's that?" Sweeney asked miserably, his elbows still on the wall, his forehead cupped in his hands.

"Nothing," Ellis said. He smiled quietly and looked up at the moon.

VIII

"Do you mind if I ask you something?" the girl said. "It's about your wife."

"Fire ahead," the traveller said gently.

They stood on the terrace in front of the hotel. Below them the sea was calm and motionless, but from behind them where the large and illuminated windows broke the blackened brick of the castle the sounds of the band came thinly.

"You haven't seen her for eight or nine years."

"Fifteen," the traveller corrected. "You needn't count the few visits between."

The girl formulated her next question carefully.

"When you married her," the girl asked, "did you love her?" The traveller's face was still moist after the dancing. She saw the small drops of sweat on his forehead while he frowned at the effort to recall the emotion of eighteen years before.

"I don't know," he answered finally. "It's funny. I can't exactly remember."

The girl looked down at the pebbles. She poked them gently with her shoe.

"I see," she said softly.

He took her hand. Then they both stood silently and watched the moon.

It rode in brilliance through the August sky. It glinted on the pebbled terrace. It stole through curtain chinks into the bedrooms of the sleeping Monsignors and Bishops, it lay in brilliant barrenness on the pillows of stiff elderly ladies who had no longer anything to dream about. Sweeney, recovering, found Ellis still gazing up at it, and joined him. It was high and radiant in the clear windy spaces of the sky. It was round and pure and white.

"*Corpus Domini Nostri*," Sweeney murmured.

Ellis straightened and dropped his cigarette end into the water below.

"Like an aspirin," he said, "like a bloody big aspirin."